A flash. A bright and powerful flash. Flames bursting up from every surface. Clothing catching fire, then hair — then skin and eyes. The magnesium casing beginning to glow white. The heat intensifying. Objects nearby now in flames as well: bedding, carpets, furniture. Within moments, the entire room is engulfed, its occupant a charred mass on a floor which itself gradually ceases to exist.

Also by Richard Weill

We Open in Oxnard Saturday Afternoon
(including the complete text of the play *Framed*)

Available from Sidney Books

LAST TRAIN TO GIDLEIGH

Last Train to Gidleigh

Richard Weill

Sidney Books

NEW YORK

www.sidneybooks.com

To contact the author, write to: RWeill@sidneybooks.com.

Interior typeface: Book Antiqua

ISBN: 978-0-9913512-8-2

First Sidney Books trade paperback edition September 2019

10 9 8 7 6 5 4 3 2 1

To my Dad, Malcolm Weill, who instilled
my love of history and detective stories;

and to Alan Spackman, my treasured
resource for all things British.

Will the bombing attacks of last autumn and winter come back again? We have proceeded on the assumption that they will.

If the lull is to end, if the storm is to renew itself, London will be ready, London will not flinch, London can take it again.

Winston Churchill
July 14, 1941

FOREWORD

Gidleigh is a small village in Devon, England. According to the 2011 census, its population is 429, which represents modest growth since the 2001 census, when its population was 428. It has a church, Holy Trinity, but no shops or school.

Nor does Gidleigh have a war memorial — unlike most of its neighboring villages — because no one from Gidleigh was killed in either the First or Second World War.

Consequently, none of the wartime story you are about to read involves anyone from Gidleigh or takes place in or near Gidleigh. None even takes place on a train to Gidleigh, as no one can travel to Gidleigh by train. Gidleigh has no railway line or railway station. The closest is Exeter St. David's, more than 20 miles away.

Then why *Last Train to Gidleigh*?

Trust that there is a reason, one that will be explained in due course. But now is not the time.

So please read on.

1. PELL GOES TO THE DETECTION CLUB

London, October 1941

Anthony Pell suddenly felt the urgent need for a great idea—a creative inspiration that excited the mind and recharged the soul. There was a time Pell's imagination reaped great ideas with the ease of one plucking fruit from a tree. But as he stood before the bedroom mirror, struggling with his black bowtie, his fruit tree was bare. And Pell could not quite recall the last harvest.

Maybe he was simply out of practice. Earlier that year, the British government began rationing paper for the duration of the war. London newspapers now had fewer editions, fewer pages, fewer copies for sale. The publication of new books was limited, too, with "essential" books prioritized. The value of popular fiction to the nation's morale notwithstanding, the government refused to consider Pell's Inspector Barnaby mysteries necessary to the war effort. So Pell had turned to writing radio dramas for the BBC to fill the void. Radio dramas required good ideas, not great ideas. Even a clever radio mystery lacked the complexity of a good Barnaby novel.

Great ideas had fueled Pell's success. His Inspector Barnaby—a Scotland Yard detective who performed amateur magic as a sideline—was a great idea. Each Inspector Barnaby mystery was the product of a great idea. Barnaby wouldn't have flourished during the 1930's—an era when every Englishman fancied himself a mystery writer—had Pell not had a head full of apparently locked rooms, seemingly impossible crimes, and initially inexplicable disappearances, each with its own, original, sensational, but entirely logical solution.

Pell feared his skills were rusting. More immediately, he feared that tonight, as he dined with his peers, he would be the only writer in the room not working on a great idea.

It had been more than a year since the Detection Club, comprised of Britain's finest mystery writers, had last gathered. Once the Blitz began in September 1940, Club president E.C. Bentley thought it best to suspend Club activities. But months had passed since a Luftwaffe bomber had last crossed the Thames. Instead of threatening Great Britain, the Germans were driving toward Moscow. The press compared it to Napoleon's Russian campaign of 1812. Would Hitler's army suffer the same fate as Napoleon's? Londoners were of two minds on this question. They prayed for a German defeat—but they feared that a retreat from Russia might mean a resumption of Hitler's designs on the British Isles.

London had endured eight months of nearly daily, then nightly, bombings. It took a long time for the city's population to accept the new reality: that the danger was over. In mid-September 1941, Bentley deemed it safe for regular Detection Club dinner meetings to resume. For all of their literary courage, mystery writers were a notoriously fearful bunch; even venturing out for the evening in a blacked-out London was often more than many could bear.

Blitz or no Blitz, London remained a blacked-out city. In the third week of October, the London sun set at about five p.m. Blackout curtains had to be closed by that hour, with not a sliver of light escaping, or an ARP warden might knock on the door with enforcement powers ranging from a warning to a legal summons.

Pell's problem was not the blackout; this evening, his curtains were well and surely closed. Tonight the problem was his black bowtie. Club dinners were formal affairs, complete with the customary red carnation in each male member's lapel. For years, Pell had depended on his wife's assistance to tie his bowtie. After all, she was the daughter of a Cambridge don, accustomed to the requirements of formal entertaining — while her husband had grown up on a Connecticut farm. Pell could tie up a horse with his eyes closed. Tying a bowtie was another matter entirely.

When the Phoney War ended in May 1940, Pell packed up Claire and the girls and shipped them off to the safety of his parents' farm in New England. They agreed that he would stay behind, at least temporarily. London was the center of his professional life. His agent was here. His publisher was here. The BBC was here. *Barnaby and the Tyburn Tree* was in galleys; *Barnaby and the Serpentine* was near completion. Talk of paper rationing was already in the air. Time was of the essence.

The Blitz began that September, and Pell started making plans to close up their Fitzrovia house and join his family. But ten days later, something happened that caused him to reconsider. The *SS City of Benares*, evacuating scores of British children to Canada, was sunk by a German U-boat. Crossing the Atlantic suddenly seemed far less safe than remaining in London. Flying was out of the question. Pell had never flown in an airplane and wasn't about to start now. As far as he was concerned, aerodynamics was on a par with alchemy.

Besides, there was also something intensely embarrassing about leaving. His friends and colleagues were too polite to say so, they might even say the opposite, but he knew that, were he to flee England now, they would never look at him the same way again.

At times, the separation was unbearable. Evenings were the most difficult. That's when he didn't have the distraction of work. That's when the absence of household activity — the eerie quiet — was most noticeable.

Then in May 1941, the Fitzrovia house suffered extensive bomb damage. It was the only London home his daughters knew. Pell wrote his best work in its spacious first-floor study. The location was ideal. BBC Broadcasting House was within walking distance. On summer evenings, the Pells could stroll to nearby Queen's Hall for the Proms.

Pell was in the Lake District when the bomb fell. He returned to find his treasured first-floor study smoldering in the back garden. Sifting through the wreckage, he thought he heard voices calling for help from under the debris. It took a moment for him to recognize the surreal voices as those of his daughters. If the structural damage hadn't forced him to relocate, his vivid imagination would have.

After a week-long search, he found charming, albeit smaller, quarters in Maida Vale.

The surrounding area fared no better than the Pells' house. Queen's Hall was destroyed. As it turned out, that May raid was the last nightly bombing. The Pell home missed surviving the Blitz by one day.

Even if the danger of relentless air raids, let alone German invasion, indeed had passed, the danger to British ships on the Atlantic had not. Just as it wasn't safe for Pell to leave, it wasn't safe for Claire and the girls to return. Many husbands and fathers were separated from their British families. The Pells would not be the exception.

Pell would have to struggle with his bowtie alone.

Several attempts later, Pell pronounced the job done. Not perfect, but done. He donned his dinner jacket, affixed his red carnation, checked the blackout curtains a final time, and departed his Maida Vale flat.

Club dinners (exclusive of the elaborate and ostentatious initiation ceremonies for new members) were held at the Garrick Club, ordinarily frequented by the leading lights of the West End. Pell had been initiated into the Detection Club five years earlier, its first American member. As a full-time Londoner, his nationality posed no barrier to admission. The Detection Club didn't care where you were born, as long as you could partake regularly in its meetings and activities.

Pell left himself extra time to get from Maida Vale to

the West End. With petrol rationing, fewer taxis were on the street at any given time. After finally finding a cab, the ride itself would take longer. Wartime headlights—blocking all but the dimmest glow—made even the most daring motorists slow down.

The near-total darkness did have one benefit. It masked the sight of two-story rubble piles, building fronts with no buildings behind, bent steel superstructures standing like carcasses stripped to their bones, and barricaded sections of missing pavement. Blitz scars were everywhere.

In the cocoon of a dark taxi, Pell's mind could continue the hunt for that elusive fresh great idea. What solution has no one used before? Who might be a "least likely suspect" *so* unlikely that no one ever considered making him—or her, or even it—the guilty party? The concept of the "least likely suspect" is something his friend Agatha Christie perfected. She'd beaten him to the punch on every category of unlikely murderer: an apparent victim, a small child, the investigating detective, even the narrator of the story. Was there anyone she hadn't used?

Then inspiration struck. Instead of searching blindly in the vast unknown, why not focus on something already known to be unknown? Instead of searching for an ill-defined idea Agatha had overlooked, why not focus on a specific problem Agatha had examined but failed to solve? Such a thing was possible, wasn't it?

***

Meanwhile, Ida Silver was looking forward to a quiet evening in her Gower Street home. She envisioned curling up with her new book, a rare find in London these days. Her husband Morris, who worked among ledgers and accounts, preferred a good play on the wireless, hopefully something funny. Every so often, for a change of pace, the two would break out a pack of cards and the cribbage board.

"Twice around the board and then off to bed," Morris would say.

How different things were from the height of the Blitz when night after night, Ida and Morris were forced to find shelter deep below the streets of Bloomsbury.

There was no wireless reception where the Silvers had huddled together on the platform of the Goodge Street tube station. The crowded conditions made it impossible to focus on anything more engaging than the evening paper. There was no space for a card game other than Scabby Queen. If you could, you slept. And you hoped you would have a home to return to in the morning.

But that ordeal finally was over. Now things could return to normal.

"We're here, guv," the taxi driver announced, stirring Pell from his reverie. They had arrived at 15 Garrick Street. Pell paid the driver and stepped onto the pavement.

"A pair of Anthonys," said a familiar voice. It was Anthony Berkeley, one of the Club's charter members. "Shall we find Lucy and make it three of a kind?" Lucy Malleson wrote mysteries under the name "Anthony Gilbert."

Berkeley and Pell entered the Garrick Club together and headed to the bar. "What is it about a war that makes a man so thirsty?" asked Berkeley.

Pell made small talk with Berkeley and the other members waiting to place their drink orders. Many expressed surprise that Pell still was in London, and had not retreated with his family to the peace of the States, with its un-rationed publishing houses. Pell could only imagine what they would have said had he, in fact, left the country.

Looking over his shoulder, Pell scanned the room searching for one person in particular. He spotted her.

"Agatha!" he said as he approached. "I was looking for you."

"Hello, Anthony," said Mrs. Christie.

"I read *Evil Under the Sun*, and wanted to congratulate you."

"Thank you, you're very kind. Is Claire still in Connecticut?"

"Yes."

"Well, you can tell her that the book should be released there any day now. Although how anyone still tolerates that insufferable bore, I'll never understand."

"Poirot?"

"Who else? I have another one coming out next month, with Tommy and Tuppence. It's been a while for those two, but at least I didn't have to write 'little grey cells' for a few months."

"I thought there was a paper shortage. Did His Majesty grant you an exemption? Are you classified as 'essential'?"

She smiled with the slightest tinge of embarrassment, suggesting that the possibility was not entirely out of the question. Pell thought it best to change the subject.

"How's Max?" he asked.

"You mean Flying Officer Max? What is it about me that makes men want to become fighter pilots?" Agatha's first husband had been an RFC pilot during the First War.

Pell tried to hide his surprise at this statement. Her friends knew not to mention Archie Christie to Agatha. Even after fifteen years, he remained a sore subject. Besides, Pell had something else he wanted to ask.

A gong sounded. Dinner was ready to be served.

"I promised Dorothy and Margery I would eat with them," Agatha said. Dorothy Sayers and Margery Allingham were waiting by the door to the dining room.

"Before you go, may I ask you a question?"

"Certainly."

"You've managed to make a murderer out of just about everyone. Is there anyone you've always wanted to have commit murder, but could never figure out how to do it?"

Agatha Christie motioned for Anthony Pell to put his ear close to her mouth, whereupon she whispered two words. He nodded that he understood.

"If you can figure it out, Anthony, my dear, the idea is all yours." She turned toward the dining room and walked away.

It was another successful Detection Club event. Even before its conclusion, the Garrick doormen would begin hailing elusive taxis to form a rank for departing Club members. Tonight this was proving to be especially difficult. The already cautious pace of nighttime London traffic had further slowed to an arthritic crawl. Through the din of honking taxi horns, Pell could hear the distinct wail of fire engine sirens. It reminded him of when fire squadrons sped through blocked streets during the Blitz. Except tonight there had been no air raid warning. Nonetheless, the unmistakable smell of smoke, coming from the direction of Bloomsbury, permeated the air.

Pell waited patiently until a taxi arrived. Waiting patiently was a British habit he had not yet acquired. Although on this occasion, he didn't mind the wait. His mind was otherwise occupied. Agatha had given him something very interesting to ponder.

2. COMPANY OFFICER HALL'S NEW ASSIGNMENT

Company Officer Keith Hall of the National Fire Service knew fires. Before the war, he had fought fires of all shapes and sizes. Then he experienced the worst days of the Blitz. Fighting Blitz fires was not his choice; he would have preferred more direct contact with the enemy, but had put off enlisting in deference to Mary and little George.

"They'll need you here, Keith," Mary had said. "You're a Leading Firefighter in the London Fire Brigade. Look at what the Germans did to Rotterdam. Soon that will be London."

After Dunkirk, he couldn't tolerate standing on the sidelines any longer. He was sent to Camp Brancepeth near Durham—but within days of the start of the Blitz, he was ordered back to his old job. From September 1940 until mid-May 1941, he spent most nights pouring water on what the Luftwaffe left behind.

"You're doing your bit as much as anyone else," Mary had said.

"I'm not fighting bloody Jerry," Keith replied. "I'm doing the washing up afterwards."

Still, he did his arduous—and dangerous—job tirelessly and with great skill, so much so that when Britain consolidated all of its local fire brigades into the National Fire Service in August 1941, Hall was promoted to the rank of Company Officer.

The last night of the Blitz, 10-11 May 1941, had been the

worst. It was not only the intensity and breadth of the fires, but also the lack of water. Water mains had been destroyed. Hoses had been laid across London to the Thames, and makeshift pumps installed.

Compared to that experience, tonight's fires were a piece of cake. Not entire sections of London in flames, just one neighborhood in Bloomsbury. Not entire streets, but scattered buildings.

Nonetheless, as he stood before the shell of one such building on Gower Street, Hall sensed something similar. It didn't take him long to realize what that thing was. It was the smell. That same burnt metallic smell that had long penetrated Hall's olfactory nerves and etched itself in his memory. People remember smells longer than they remember sights or sounds — and Hall would not soon forget the metallic smell that so marked the Blitz fires he had fought for eight months, from the white hot magnesium cylinder in German incendiary bombs.

Ordinary fires did not smell like Blitz fires, and Hall had enough experience with both to tell the difference.

During the Blitz, incendiary bombs were a fixture in London nightlife. Weather permitting, "fireraisers" rained daily from Junker and Heinkel bombers, often housed in a "Göring bread basket" containing hundreds at a time.

But those raids had ended five months ago. The Luftwaffe had changed directions, flying east against the Soviet Union. And they had not returned.

In those five months, the NFS never had to fight as

many fires in one night as it was fighting tonight. Several
buildings on Gower Street were engulfed in flames, and Company Officer Hall knew of reports of similar blazes throughout
Bloomsbury. The British Museum was safe, he'd been told. The
fires were all in residential buildings. All were intense and had
gone out of control immediately. But, most unusually, no two
were together. One here, one there — not like in the Blitz, when
a "bread basket" rained incendiaries on one location, setting
every building in the area ablaze. This was not the case
tonight.

Hall wondered about the smell of the other fires.

He wondered about another thing, too. Even as this
magnesium-smelling fire destroyed one Gower Street home —
and other fires destroyed dozen of other buildings throughout
Bloomsbury — the skies over London remained free of Junkers,
Heinkels, and bread baskets.

Tonight there was no raid.

The following morning, Morris Silver, wrapped in a
gray wool blanket, sat in silence on the Gower Street pavement across the road from what little remained of his house.
As he watched, an ARP stretcher party combed through the
wreckage of last night's fire, looking for Morris' wife Ida. She
was upstairs when the fire started; he was downstairs. She
didn't answer when he called to her, so he tried to mount the
staircase, but the smoke and flames were too intense. Finally,
he escaped to the street, hoping she'd done the same. When

the ARP party returned bearing a full stretcher, he knew that she hadn't.

That night, Hall and his NFS crew were back in Bloomsbury, fighting several additional fires. It was the same pattern as the night before—only the fires were fewer in number. Over the next several days, the fires continued, although there were fewer and fewer with each passing day. Five days after the Bloomsbury fires began, they stopped entirely.

Yet the smell of burning magnesium remained. Hall was confused. These were Blitz fires with no Blitz.

Home Secretary Herbert Morrison's copy of the *Daily Express* lay unopened on his desk. The front-page headline was all Morrison needed to see: "Silent Blitz Strikes London Again." A week after the Bloomsbury fires, a similar pattern of fires destroyed several dozen residential buildings dotting Knightsbridge: a rash of fires the first night, then fewer and fewer on subsequent nights. Londoners were back on edge. Soon the Prime Minister would be calling, and the Home Secretary would need answers for him.

Morrison picked up his telephone. "Get me Firebrace at the NFS."

Aylmer Firebrace's official title was Chief of the Fire Staff and Inspector-in-Chief of the National Fire Service. A naval officer in the First War, he had been Commander of the

London Fire Brigade during the Blitz. When the bombings ceased in May 1941, Firebrace was sent to the Home Office to work on plans for a nationwide fire service. One of those plans must have included giving the National Fire Service's commander the highfalutin title of Chief of Fire Staff and Inspector-in-Chief—and to take this title for himself. No one complained. Firebrace was an iconic figure. Earlier that year, the King bestowed him with the honor of Commander of the Order of the British Empire.

But now Firebrace had a new problem. It wasn't enough that the NFS put the fires out. Now the Home Office was insisting that he determine what got them started.

"We're not a bleedin' police department," Firebrace had told the Home Secretary. "If it's arson, then it's Scotland Yard's business. If it's sabotage, then it's a matter for MI5."

"We don't know what it is, Aylmer," replied Morrison. "Winston will want this stopped, and your people know fires. We're not asking you to go around arresting people. Just conduct an examination of the scenes and file a report."

Firebrace knew when to step back and follow orders. He requisitioned the roster and personnel files of his most experienced men. One name caught his eye. Why was that? Ah, yes, Firebrace thought, that's the lad who keeps asking to go back into the Army. He can't wait to go toe-to-toe with the enemy. Firebrace opened the man's personnel file: an excellent NFS officer, an up-and-comer. Why the hell not? It wasn't as if anyone else in London had experience with this sort of thing.

"Gladys," he called to his secretary, "locate Company Officer Keith Hall and tell him to come see me on the double!"

"With all due respect, sir, doesn't that require specialized training?" Keith Hall stood before his commanding officer, a bit stunned by what he had just been asked to do.

"Rubbish," said Aylmer Firebrace. "You know fires. You know how fires spread. Your ability to deploy your men depends on you knowing how fires spread."

"Yes, but how does that—?"

"You work backwards. You apply the same knowledge in reverse. Not where a fire is going, but where it came from."

Hall was dubious, but kept his doubts to himself. Firebrace had been a Navy man. The Royal Navy was all about every man doing his duty. He was now being asked to do his.

"What exactly am I supposed to determine?" he asked.

"As much as you can," Firebrace replied. "Select two good men to accompany you. Make sure one can operate a camera so you can document what you find. And be careful. Whatever is still standing in those buildings is surely ready to collapse."

Hall thanked his commander for the warning and departed quietly. What had he gotten himself into? Something different, at least. Not only that, but something of interest to the Home Secretary, and maybe even the Prime Minister. Perhaps Mary was right. Perhaps he was serving the war effort after all.

3. PELL GOES TO WORK

Anthony Pell owed the BBC a script, but elected instead to spend the morning musing over the "Christie problem," as he'd begun to call it.

Pell thought he knew the secret to mystery writing. It didn't matter whether one was writing a book, or for the radio, or the stage. The secret was to identify and exploit the reader's (or audience's) expectations. For example, if you are writing an English country house mystery—a murder in a closed society with everyone a suspect—the reader opens the book already expecting links between the victim and each of the characters, with each also having a convincing motive to kill. The reader ignores how utterly improbable this basic situation is, because it is exactly what the reader expects. No one asks: "You mean *everyone* present has a different reason to kill the same person? How often does that happen?" They know it happens *all the time* in books like this. It ceases to be unusual. Is it any wonder these readers are stunned to learn that instead of one guilty party among multiple suspects, there were multiple guilty parties and *no* innocent suspects—a far more logical outcome had their expectations not interfered?

In Pell's signature specialty, the locked-room mystery, the reader knows to focus on door locks and bolts, window bars, and lit fireplaces. Finding ways to pass through a bolted door, a barred window, or down a smoke-filled chimney are the conventions of the genre. And since a locked-room mystery is naturally theatrical, one or two stray theatre references are certainly expected and will hardly be noticed. So while the reader is pondering whether the door really did remain in the line of sight of the unimpeachable witness for the entire period in question, Pell bypasses the doors, windows, and fireplaces entirely — and has the killer enter through the floor. ("Of course! It's an old stage floor with a trap door. Didn't someone say that the building was once a theatre?")

Radio is no different. Every audience member expects that radio actors will be playing multiple parts using different voices. They never assume, when they hear the same voice altered slightly for a second role, that it's the same character returning in disguise. So exploit that fact. Just like stage audiences know that, when a character dies on stage, the actor isn't really dead. But, for some reason, they never think: maybe the character isn't either.

Identifying and exploiting expectations — that's all it is.

For Inspector Barnaby — Pell's fictional detective — finding the secret to a locked-room murder or seemingly impossible crime was no different than discerning the secret to a mind-boggling magic trick. Barnaby's experience in, and understanding of, the various ways a magician fools his audience was his special skill, his edge. Magicians also exploit expectations. That's why Pell and his creation were a perfect match.

But the "Christie problem" confounded everything Pell thought he knew about writing mysteries. He was prepared for something like this. After all, Agatha Christie knew a bit about writing mysteries, too, and this problem had confounded her first.

Pell needed a new approach. When an answer continued to elude him, Pell scoured the morning newspapers, hoping some recent item might provide inspiration. The papers were all abuzz over the "Silent Blitz." The night before, Islington was the target.

But no brilliant idea materialized from the day's headlines. It was a long shot, he should have realized, and long shots rarely paid off.

Pell's secretary, Mildred Tate, knew enough not to bother her employer at moments like this. She busied herself quietly with gathering and opening the post—delivered promptly at 9:00 a.m. and 2:00 p.m. daily—organizing the correspondence that required a response, paying bills, and preparing royalty checks for deposit. Noisily typing letters and script pages could wait until Pell either emerged from his state of rumination or took his contemplation for a walk.

Until her departure for America, Claire Pell always handled these things for her husband. After she left, he considered hiring a secretary, but the war made secretaries scarce. Employment agencies closed, having no one to employ.

In December 1940, Pell finally reached the breaking point. Pell never knew the torture of writing and addressing Christmas cards before Christmas 1940, and he swore never to undertake this ordeal on his own again.

Four days after that Christmas, the Germans launched

their largest raid of the Blitz. Much of the attack centered on St. Paul's Cathedral. Incendiary bombs pierced the church dome and started fires below. There were radio reports that the church had been destroyed, but in truth the St. Paul's Watch, a tireless band of volunteers dedicated to protecting the cathedral, put the fires out. Nearby Paternoster Row, center of many London publishing houses, had not been so lucky. The offices of such publishers as Hutchinson, Collins, and Longmans were destroyed. Wholesale book distributor Simpkin Marshall's warehouse was seriously damaged, with five million volumes lost. Few enough books were in circulation; this made matters worse.

Mildred Tate had worked for Simpkin Marshall for 38 years, but the effect of the 29 December bombing proved too great for the business to survive. She was out of a job by April. At 61 years of age, she had few opportunities. All of her connections were in Paternoster Row—what was left of it. But in June, she learned through a friend that Anthony Pell, now resettled in Maida Vale, was looking for a secretary.

She and Pell hit it off immediately.

"What the deuce are you doing out of uniform?" he joked.

"If I were presumptuous, I could ask the same of you, Mr. Pell."

"I have an excuse. I'm an American."

"Then why aren't you in America?"

"Because I'm also a Londoner. Lived here for twelve

years."

"Just visiting?"

"Actually, I came for the atmosphere. The London fog, you might say. Thought it would help my writing. And though I couldn't find a hansom cab to save my life, it did help. So I stayed, met my wife here, became a Londoner. But still an American."

It took the two a few weeks to work out the routine. Pell's forced move from Fitzrovia to Maida Vale had made things infinitely more complicated. The Maida Vale flat was close quarters for Pell and a secretary to work together without interference. Coordinating in the small space had its challenges. But four months later, it was all second nature. Mildred knew what not to do when Pell was thinking, sensitive to distraction, and what she could do when he was too absorbed in his writing to hear anything else.

This morning, Pell was thinking. Finished with her quiet work, Mildred waited patiently until Pell took his thinking outside. He could have taken the "Christie problem" up to Kilburn Park. Instead, he walked down Abbey Road toward Lord's Cricket Ground in St. John's Wood, avoiding the bomb damage on nearby Abercorn Place and Grove End Road. He rarely took notes or jotted down ideas on these walks. If an idea wasn't good enough to remember, it wasn't good enough. The mind was a great editor.

By the time he returned hours later, Mildred had finished her typing. Letters were ready for his signature; retyped

BBC script pages were ready for his review.

But the "Christie problem" remained unsolved. In frustration, Pell grabbed the retyped BBC script from Mildred's desk. "Might as well finish this today," he said. He was unenthusiastic. To Pell, once the details of a story were in place, the rest followed easily. All the hard work was done. But easily doesn't mean joyfully. Pell's joy was in the planning.

As soon as Pell disappeared inside his small workroom, Mildred went to the kitchen and put the kettle on the hob. She sensed Pell's disquietude. A cup of tea would do him a world of good.

4. HALL FILES HIS REPORT

To: Chief of Fire Staff and Inspec-
          tor-in-Chief Aylmer Firebrace
From: Company Officer Keith Hall
Subject: "Silent Blitz" Fires
Date: 12 November 1941

As instructed, I have examined and photographed fire scenes in Bloomsbury, Knightsbridge, and Islington, all victims of the so-called "Silent Blitz." I was accompanied by two members of the National Fire Service, Section Leader Leonard Tomlinson and Leading Fireman Bennett Weston. Our findings are as follows:

1. We saw no incendiary devices. None of the scenes revealed the steel tail-and-fin pieces commonly found in the wreckage of a German incendiary bomb. However, we did notice the same distinct odor of burnt magnesium that accompanied the incendiary fires of the 1940-1941 Blitz.

2. We found no evidence of explosives. No survivors in or near the damaged buildings recall hearing any noise at the time to suggest an explosion. (This fact has been discussed at length in the newspapers, and is the principal reason why this rash of fires has been nicknamed the "Silent Blitz.")

3. All fires appear to have originated in occupied residential dwellings. None

was started in commercial premises; none
was started in a vacant building.

4. Some buildings could not be examined because their superstructure was completely consumed by fire. Where this did
not occur, the building's upper floors received a great deal more fire damage than
the ground floor. We believe that these
fires started above the ground floor.

5. ARP Stretcher Parties removed the
bodies of all fire victims before we made
our examination. Accordingly, we do not
know their precise location in the premises. We were told that each body was burned
beyond recognition, and could only be
identified circumstantially.

6. According to witnesses, even fires
that started within hours of each other
did not begin simultaneously. This is consistent with our failure to find any timing devices in the affected buildings.

7. We doubt that these fires were
started by someone throwing an object into
the building. First, many fires appear to
have started above the ground floor. Second, blackout curtains would have made it
impossible to throw an object well into
the building's interior, especially on an
upper floor. Third, while we encountered
many broken windows, they seemed to have
broken out (from the fire), not in (from a
thrown object).

8. Nor does it appear that anyone

broke into any of the affected buildings. Each dwelling was locked. There is no evidence of tampering with any door or window lock. Whatever started these fires either originated within the building or entered with an occupant's consent.

Aylmer Firebrace read Hall's report with the officer standing silently in front of his desk. "Strike the references to 'Silent Blitz.' The Home Secretary hates that name. And don't quote the newspapers. If we wanted a report of what's in the newspapers, we wouldn't need you."

"Do you have a better name, sir?"

"You needn't give anything a name. We're not selling shaving soap. Identify the fires by their date and location."

"Yes, sir."

"And thank you, Hall. You did a good job under difficult circumstances."

"Excuse me, sir, but—am I through with this assignment, once I fix the report, that is? I mean, if there's anything else you want me to do—"

"No need, Hall. This is a police matter now. A point I will make very clear to the Home Office."

"I just thought—"

"And good thinking it was, too, lad."

The Home Secretary waited until the other Cabinet members left the room and he was left alone with the Prime Minister. He handed Churchill the short typewritten memorandum. "This is from Firebrace."

"About Max's 'Silent Blitz'?" Max Aitken, known officially as Lord Beaverbrook—one of Churchill's oldest friends, formerly Minister of Aircraft Production, and now Minister of Supply—published the *Daily Express*.

"I hate that name."

Churchill began to read. "Pretty skimpy, don't you think? It says more about what didn't happen than what did."

"Aylmer's people aren't arson investigators, Winston."

"Arson? This isn't arson. Not on this scale. No, this is sabotage."

"Should I pass it along to David Petrie, then?" Petrie was the new Director General of MI5.

"Petrie's a typical Scot: strong as an ox, righteous as a saint, but with the imagination of burnt toast. But I know just the man." Churchill picked up the phone. "Miss Layton, get me Raymond Mott at MI5."

"You can't do that!"

"Why not?"

"Chain of command."

"If I'd followed chain of command, Halifax would be sitting in this chair, and not me."

"Ring off, please, Winston. Let me deal with Petrie. I'll get this into Mott's hands without ruffling any feathers."

"Feathers need a good ruffling every now and again."

But Churchill did what the Home Secretary asked. In truth, he appreciated having one less problem to manage.

5. COLONEL MOTT TAKES CHARGE

Colonel Raymond Mott showed no surprise when Director General Petrie relayed the Prime Minister's directive. He'd been following the "Silent Blitz" closely in the press, and assumed this day would soon come. And, although he kept this part to himself, he already had begun forming a plan for the assignment. This was a new kind of investigation; it needed a new kind of investigator.

Mott had been Chief of Special Operations at MI5 longer than anyone could remember. MI5 Directors General came and went—Petrie, the current DG, was the third to occupy the top office at 57-58 St. James's Street in less than two years—but Raymond Mott was an MI5 fixture.

Mott's specialty was personnel recruitment: marshaling people with special talents for special jobs, within MI5 and without. Great Britain's unique culture nurtured unique skills. Many could be adapted to aid the nation's survival. For example, the codebreakers stationed at Bletchley Park's Government Code and Cypher School originally had been drawn exclusively from the Cambridge and Oxford mathematics departments—until, that is, one Sunday afternoon, when Mott watched in amazement as his nephew breezed through the cryptic clues in *The Times* crossword. Mott envisioned applying the peculiar mental acuity of Britain's best crossword solvers, including those far better than his nephew, to the task of decoding encrypted transmissions. Here was an untapped national resource, and untapped resources were something Britain could ill afford to waste.

Later he watched British illusionist Jasper Maskelyne deceive an audience at St. George's Hall, and suggested to the Army that it put the country's finest stage magicians to work camouflaging ships, tanks, and entire military installations. He also encouraged MI6 to recruit West End actors to portray foreign nationals.

The "Silent Blitz" spawned a new idea—a new cache of distinctively British talent he could mold to further the war effort. For obvious reasons, one name in particular stood out above the rest; ironically, he wasn't even British. Mott reached across his large oak desk, picked up the telephone, and dialed.

Hours later, Anthony Pell stood across the great oak desk. "I'd like to know what this is about," he said, using confrontation to deflect the anxiety of the moment.

Mott relit his pipe with a silver lighter and took a long draw. "What do you think it's about?"

"Well, let's see. I'm home working, minding my own business, when two men I don't know order me to accompany them for reasons I'm not told. Have I won a sweepstakes?"

"Americans have such a wonderful way of mixing outrage with irony."

"And the British have such a charming way of masking arrogance with politeness."

"Is this a trait your wife shares?"

Mott's remark took Pell by surprise. "Obviously, you know more about me than I know about you," he said.

"Our motto at MI5. Why don't you sit down?" Mott motioned to the hardwood chair near where Pell was standing.

"I'm not sure I want to." Pell paused. "MI5. That's like the British secret police, right?"

"Military intelligence. The domestic side. As opposed to MI6, which handles overseas operations."

"This can't be because of something I put in a radio script. All the scripts are approved by the Ministry of Information." Pell paused. "Is it something I didn't include?" he asked.

"Mr. Pell, you have a keen, logical mind."

"A coded message to British agents on the Continent? You know, 'Listen to the BBC at ten p.m. If you hear the sentence, "My uncle breeds dogs in Madagascar," then blow up the railway line between Paris and Marseilles'?"

"If there are any British agents on the Continent, and I'm not saying one way or another, they're the province of MI6."

"How discreet of you."

"Our other motto," said Mott, relighting his pipe yet again. "They say you're also quite a clever man, Mr. Pell."

"They tell me that, too."

"One who might prove very useful to us. How do you feel about helping us beat the Germans? Or are you a religiously neutral American?"

"I'm not religious at all."

"And your family is British. British but living in America, while you, an American, remain here. Why is that?"

"Sometimes I wonder," Pell replied reflexively. He had no intention of discussing his deepest fears with this stranger — his fear of flying, of U-boat wolfpacks, of his peers looking at him askance. "Our home was here until a German bomber found it. My professional roots are here. I don't know if I could write in the States. Never did very well at it before."

"Mr. Pell, this country needs clever people."

"I'm sure you have many of them, Colonel."

"Yes, but too many of them think alike. Grew up together, trained together, went to the same schools, read the same books, have the same ideas. One can't surprise the other. All peas in the same pod. You're different. You approach problems from odd angles. You're unpredictable. You didn't read the book, you wrote it."

"The books are fiction, Colonel."

"A clever idea is a clever idea, no matter where it appears." Mott puffed vigorously on his pipe to keep the tobacco glowing red. "This country is fighting for its life. We have to mine every resource we have. We've adapted every special skill we possess for the cause. Clever mystery writers are a unique British resource, and not just for writing coded messages in radio scripts. Any idiot can do that."

"Doing what then?"

Mott paused. "Pell, what I'm about to say is highly confidential. I'm only telling you because I need your help. I trust you will keep what I say in the strictest confidence."

"All right," said Pell.

"Are you familiar with the 'Silent Blitz' fires?" asked Mott.

"No, I've been living in a cave since St. Swithin's Day."

"The Prime Minister wants them stopped. He's ordered me to put a team together for that purpose. It will include members of the National Fire Service, Scotland Yard's Special Branch, and MI5."

"Good luck."

"This past May, after the German battleship *Bismark* sank the *HMS Hood*, the Prime Minister ordered the Admiralty to sink the *Bismark*. He told them, 'I don't care how you do it.' Well, I've now been given much the same instruction as the Admiralty received in May."

"I don't know anything about fires."

"They're not just fires, Mr. Pell. Something is passing through locked doors and windows and igniting inside dozens of nearby buildings, most on the same night. It's a locked-room problem. You're precisely the man to figure out how it's done."

"Don't be so sure, Colonel. Remember—I don't figure out locked-room problems, I create them. There's a difference. Some people can watch a magician and know instantly how the trick is done. I only know how the trick is done if I designed the trick."

"You underestimate yourself."

"Do I? A few weeks ago, another Detection Club member gave me a problem to work on. I'm no closer to an answer now than I was when I began. And it's not for lack of trying."

"So take a crack at our little problem instead. As a change of pace. For all of our sakes."

"Let me think about it."

"We haven't the time for indecision."

"I'm sorry, but I have to think about it."

"Then think quickly, please."

The next night, the 'Silent Blitz' struck Kew. The following morning, Mott rang Pell's home, but Mildred said Pell was out for a walk. Mott didn't believe her, but there was nothing he could do about it. He thought fleetingly of asking the Prime Minister to enlist President Roosevelt's assistance. FDR was known to be quite an admirer of Pell's work. But Mott couldn't envision America's Neutrality Act permitting the U.S. President to pressure an American citizen to fight for Britain.

6. Dorothy Tanner Gets an Opportunity

The initial members of Mott's task force were Keith Hall's NFS team—Hall, Leonard Tomlinson, and Bennett Weston; Sergeant Stuart MacDonald from Special Branch; and Mott's deputy, Giles Curtis.

Curtis questioned including the NFS men. "We need spooks and coppers," he said. "They're neither."

"Studied many fires, Giles?" Mott asked. "I haven't. No one in Special Branch has. No one at Box 500 has." Box 500 was the insiders' term for MI5; its official address was PO Box 500, London W2. "These guys know fires."

"Then give me Hall. We don't need all three."

"Hall needs Tomlinson and Weston when going in the buildings. Those places are deathtraps. So even if they're as useful as a chocolate teapot in meetings, they stay. I want everyone connected with this investigation under one roof. For security reasons." Mott drew on his pipe and shuffled some random papers for a moment before proposing an additional name. "What about Dorothy Tanner?" he asked.

"Tanner's a file clerk," Curtis replied.

"That's because Petrie won't give her anything more challenging to do. She got very high marks at Beaulieu," the Hampshire MI5 training facility.

"She has no experience."

"She's very bright," said Mott.

Curtis shrugged. If Mott wanted to cut his own throat,

Curtis wouldn't stop him. "You're the boss," was all he said.

Dorothy Tanner joined MI5 in the spring of 1939, four months before the war began. After completing her training, she expected to serve her country in time of war in a meaningful way. Instead, she had been given an office clerical assignment. She did her job efficiently and without complaint, while also letting her superiors know that she was equally willing to tackle something more urgent, more dangerous even. Raymond Mott made a mental note of Dorothy's overtures. He was fairly certain that if he could accommodate Dorothy, she would return his loyalty.

"I'm assigning you to the 'Silent Blitz' task force," Mott told her. Dorothy wondered if she had heard him correctly.

"Me?" she asked. She could feel her heart race.

"Yes, you. Officially, your responsibility is to assist Giles, who is our principal representative. Unofficially, your responsibility is to ensure that I know exactly what the task force is doing. I don't trust Special Branch. I have no confidence in the investigative capabilities of the National Fire Service. And, between us, I have no doubt that Giles Curtis would stab me in the back at his first opportunity. I need someone in the room I can rely on. Someone who will be my eyes and ears. And something tells me you're my person. Am I wrong?"

"No, sir," Dorothy said with a smile. "Thank you. I won't let you down."

***

The "Silent Blitz" team gathered around a large wooden table in a cleared-out storeroom at 57-58 St. James's Street. For security reasons, Mott chose a room with no windows. The residual stale odor of old files was not his concern.

There were six chairs—for Giles Curtis and Dorothy Tanner of MI5; Stuart MacDonald of Special Branch; and Keith Hall, Leonard Tomlinson, and Bennett Weston of the National Fire Service. In front of each chair was a manila folder containing Hall's NFS reports together with Weston's photographs.

Giles Curtis set the tone: "We have a very specific mission. Determine who is setting these fires. Apprehend them. Interrogate them. Identify who is directing them, from whom they are getting their supplies, and with whom they are working. Then we either turn them or hang them."

Giles let his message linger in the room's stagnant air. MacDonald drew a Woodbine cigarette from its pack, intent on replacing the pervasive mustiness with the sweet smell of tar. After a few respectful seconds, he asked his question: "Where did the bodies go? There's nothing here about the location and condition of the bodies."

"They were all gone by the time we got there," Hall answered. "That's standard ARP procedure. A rescue team looks for survivors while a stretcher party removes the dead."

"Bollocks," said MacDonald. "This is a criminal investigation. Knowing whether the body was near where the fire started, or in another part of the house, is critical."

"I'll look into changing the procedure," said Hall.

"Meaning we have to wait for more fires?" MacDonald said derisively. Hall didn't take the bait.

"What else do we have to go on?" Giles Curtis asked.

"As I've said from that first night in Bloomsbury, they must have used an incendiary device much like the incendiary bombs the Jerrys used to drop," said Hall. "I'm telling you, all of these fires smell exactly like Blitz fires." Tomlinson and Weston nodded their agreement. "It's the burning magnesium," Hall added.

"Other than magnesium, what does an incendiary bomb contain?" Curtis asked.

"Thermite," said Hall. "Thermite in a magnesium shell backed by a steel tail with three steel fins."

"But no steel components were found here, correct? And they would have survived the fires."

"No tails, no fins, but you don't need either if you're not dropping a bomb from thousands of feet up. The rest—the thermite and magnesium—burns up."

"If you're throwing the device through a window, you do need a casing strong enough to hold the bleedin' thing together," MacDonald said.

"They weren't thrown in. Not like a grenade, I mean," said Leonard Tomlinson. "Some fires started upstairs, in the back of the house."

"Any theories how the devices got inside?" Giles asked. No one answered.

"What struck me, from your reports, Mr. Hall, was the

absence of a pattern," said Dorothy at last. Giles shifted in his chair and gave her a sharp glance. He did not welcome her unschooled contribution. Undeterred, she went on: "Put yourself in the place of the saboteur. You're bent on destroying dozens of homes in a confined area on the same night. You must be quick and efficient. Which means finding a quick, efficient, and effective way to get the incendiaries inside each building. Maybe it's throwing them through the window —"

"They just said that —" Giles interrupted.

"You're missing my point, Mr. Curtis," Dorothy continued. "As I was saying, you might consider throwing them through the window. Or climbing up on the roof and dropping them down the chimney. Or shoving them up a drainpipe. The chosen method doesn't matter."

"It doesn't?" Giles said, in a tone that made little effort to conceal his incredulity.

"No. What matters is that, having found a quick, efficient, and effective way to get the incendiaries inside each building — whatever it is — doesn't it follow that you would use the same method for every building? That there would be a consistent pattern? I see no pattern."

"Miss Tanner's correct. There's no pattern," Hall said.

"Which means what?" Giles asked.

"A variable," said MacDonald. "I agree with Miss Tanner. The saboteur would follow a set routine. The job is too dangerous, too difficult. He'd find one way that works and stick to it. If instead it went off in all different directions, it must mean a new element was introduced. Where the saboteur left off. A variable."

"The homeowner," said Dorothy. "That's a variable that differs from house to house."

"The saboteur gave the device to the homeowner?" Giles asked.

"It's a reasonable hypothesis," MacDonald replied. "It fits what we know."

"So the device was in a milk bottle, delivered by the milkman?" Giles asked.

MacDonald smiled. "I think you've solved it, Mr. Curtis." Giles didn't return the smile. "At least that's the general idea," MacDonald said.

"We had our first meeting," Dorothy reported, "and concluded that the Metropolitan Police should stop anyone unfamiliar delivering parcels. And the public warned not to accept parcels of unknown origin."

"Do you have any evidence that this is how these fires were started?" Mott asked.

"It's a theory," said Dorothy. "But the best we have."

"It's almost December, Miss Tanner. Do you really think I can get the whole of London to stop accepting surprise parcels? Besides, a warning will compromise our operation."

"Don't we have a higher duty to the public?"

Mott sighed. "I'll take it to the Home Secretary," he said.

7. THE POSTMAN AND THE BAT

Neither knew the other's name. It was safer that way. One worked outside. He was "The Postman" for obvious reasons. He delivered the goods, both literally and figuratively. The other worked inside. He was "The Bat" because, well, he was blind. The Bat's blindness was not a disability but an occupational necessity. Essential to the operation's success was The Bat's ability to make his contribution in the dark.

Berlin had supplied rolls of magnesium sheeting and canisters of chlorine dioxide through a network of Abwehr agents stationed in Britain, although none knew The Postman or The Bat's true identity or whereabouts either. Only one contact—the one who chose their locations, designed the device, and instructed them on construction and deployment—knew who they were. But for similar security reasons, The Postman and The Bat didn't know him.

The mission was to restore some semblance of disquiet into the London psyche, at least until the Luftwaffe could resume more massive attacks. Hitler and Göring were displeased by reports of Londoners returning to normal civilian life, and ordered Admiral Canaris, chief of the Abwehr, to do something to disrupt the calm.

The Postman and The Bat read with pride Fleet Street headlines proclaiming the "Silent Blitz." They hoped Canaris also would be pleased, and Göring, and maybe even the Führer.

Privately, The Postman and The Bat never called what they were doing the "Silent Blitz." To them it was the "Blitz auf die billige": the "Blitz on the cheap." It was the equivalent of using Kriegsmarine frogmen in the place of a U-boat wolf-pack.

They knew that the longer their mission lasted, the harder it would be to achieve widespread success. They already had lost the element of surprise. Police presence in residential neighborhoods had increased. Bobbies were checking uniformed Royal Mail postmen. The BBC was warning Londoners against opening unexpected parcels.

The Postman and The Bat agreed that the ultimate success of their mission required that they suspend operations temporarily. Hopefully, Admiral Canaris, Reichsmarschall Göring, the Führer—not to mention their mysterious contact—would understand.

8. 'ALVAR LIDELL READING IT'

London, December 1941

Anthony Pell hated Sundays. Sundays were too quiet for productive work. Productive work required a modest level of ambient noise: gentle footsteps, shuffling papers, banal conversation. Nothing loud, nothing sharp—such as the crisp keystrokes on Mildred's typewriter. Mildred's other busywork around the house, however, served splendidly. But, of course, Mildred was not around on Sundays.

The BBC Home Service often provided the necessary ambiance. The continuous, predictable programming that filled the daytime hours supplied a perfect background. But Sundays, religious programs dominated, and Pell found these more distracting than insulating.

Fortunately, this Sunday, Pell had no pressing assignments. His most recent BBC script was scheduled for broadcast the following Friday evening at eight p.m. He had a few days to relax, write to Claire and the girls, and take long walks to muse over the "Christie problem," something always lingering in his consciousness.

And at six and nine p.m., Pell made sure he tuned in to the BBC's Sunday evening news broadcasts.

"This is the BBC Home Service. Here is the news, and this is Alvar Lidell reading it. Japan's long-threatened aggression in the Far

East began tonight with air attacks on United States naval bases in the Pacific. Fresh reports are coming in every minute. The latest facts of the situation are these: Messages from Tokyo say that Japan has announced a formal declaration of war against both United States and Britain.

"Japan's attacks on American naval bases in the Pacific were announced by President Roosevelt in a statement from the White House tonight. The first statement said that the naval base of Pearl Harbor and other naval and military targets in the chief Hawaiian island of Oahu had been attacked from the air. Almost immediately after, came the announcement that Manila in the Philippines had also been raided.

"A little while ago, Mr. Stephen Early, White House press secretary, said that as far as was known at the moment, the attacks were still going on. In other words, he said, we do not know the Japanese have bombed and left.

"Acting on his executive authority, President Roosevelt has ordered the mobilization of the United States Army, and given instructions to both the Army and the Navy to carry out undisclosed orders prepared for the defense of the United States.

"So much for the official news. . . ."

Pell's first thoughts were of Claire and his daughters, forgetting momentarily the non-existent possibility of a Japanese air attack on Torrington, Connecticut. Nonetheless, the patina of their complete safety was gone.

Pell's next thought was of Colonel Mott. Suddenly, his

perspective on assisting the war effort had changed. Granted, it was highly unlikely that the Japanese also had orchestrated the "Silent Blitz" fires, but war was war. The United States was surely in it now. No more Lending; no more Leasing; in all the way. The least he could do was figure out a locked-room problem for them.

Mott was pleased to receive Pell's call Monday morning, but not surprised. At 12:30 p.m. that afternoon Washington time, President Roosevelt was addressing a joint session of the U.S. Congress. It was widely reported that he would seek at least a declaration of war against Japan (or perhaps the entire Axis, depending on overnight developments) — and Congressional leaders already had made it clear that FDR could expect to receive unanimous support for his request.

Pell arrived at 57-58 St. James's Street shortly thereafter. Sandbags remained piled along the building's façade to protect the entrance from bombs exploding at close range (for nothing can protect against a direct hit with a high explosive). A uniformed officer waited for Pell just inside the street door and escorted him to Mott's office upstairs.

There Mott briefed Pell on the task force's current theory, in the same detail Dorothy Tanner had reported it to him. Mott then summoned Giles Curtis, introduced Pell, and advised Giles of Pell's special assignment. Curtis' face betrayed even less enthusiasm for this announcement than the news of Dorothy's addition to the team.

"What his problem?" Pell asked after Curtis left the room.

"He's old school. You've heard of thinking inside the box versus outside the box? Giles not only thinks inside the box, but the box he thinks inside is an 18th century sea chest."

Pell sensed his meeting was over and turned to leave.

"One last thing," Mott added, holding out a formal-looking document and a fountain pen. "The Official Secrets Act."

"What's that?"

"A document you sign whereby you acknowledge your understanding that if you communicate any official secret without lawful authority, you are committing a crime and could go to prison for up to two years. And that's only if you tell your mother or your maiden aunt. If you tell someone who turns out to be working for the enemy — well, let's just say that the rope-making factory in Charlton doesn't work round-the-clock only for the benefit of the Royal Navy."

"But you wouldn't interfere with a poor writer practicing his craft, would you? In other words, after I solve your locked-room problem, I would get to write about it, wouldn't I?" Pell said with a smile.

"What do you think?" said Mott, his face solemn as stone.

9. Pell Speaks Up

Anthony Pell had been right all along. Solving someone else's locked-room problem is harder than designing your own. When designing your own, you needn't account for the vagaries of human nature. People will do what you have them do. You can even bend the laws of nature, as long as you artfully justify the reasons to your readers. Readers who are eager to believe.

Reality, on the other hand, can smart like a cold shower. The "Silent Blitz" team already had developed a persuasive theory that incendiary devices, later consumed by fire, were delivered to residents of the target buildings who, in turn, took them to random locations inside: different floors, different rooms on those floors. But what ignited these devices?

Most of the fires started after dark. Was this when the parcels were delivered, or did the device include some feature that delayed their ignition? What about the fires that did not begin until the next day or several days later?

And why had the fires stopped? After clusters in Bloomsbury, Knightsbridge, Islington, and Kew, each spaced days apart, two weeks had passed with no new fires. Had the enhanced police patrols and BBC public warnings sent the saboteur underground? Or—was it possible that one of the Kew bodies burned beyond recognition (and removed prematurely from the fire scene by an ARP stretcher party) was all that remained of the saboteur?

No one wanted the "Silent Blitz" to continue—but stopping the fires was only one part of the team's mission. A dead saboteur couldn't be interrogated and turned against the other members of his espionage network.

Pell was extraordinarily self-conscious that, among his fellow task-force members, he was the lone amateur. Yes, he had Raymond Mott's endorsement, but Mott's deputy, Giles Curtis, made no secret of his view that this investigation was the province of professionals, not "spinners of fairy tales." Stuart MacDonald of the Yard's Special Branch was only slightly less resistant to Pell. In contrast, no one on Keith Hall's NFS team seemed particularly bothered by Pell's presence; after all, NFS personnel weren't criminal investigators either.

Only Dorothy Tanner actually welcomed Pell warmly. Pell attributed this to Curtis' obvious, equal disdain for Dorothy. Clearly, she welcomed someone with whom to share the doghouse. He didn't yet know the other reason Dorothy accepted Pell as readily as she did: of all the task-force members, Miss Tanner was the most loyal to Colonel Mott; his choice of Anthony Pell was good enough for her.

What made this internal caste system so odd to Pell was the evident fact that *no one* on the "Silent Blitz" task force knew much about the science of arson investigation. MI5 knew a lot about finding German saboteurs operating in Britain and turning spies into double agents. Special Branch knew a lot about investigating homicides and political subversives. The National Fire Service knew how to fight a fire and assess the structural integrity of whatever remained. But none of the discussion around the large wooden table in the work room at 57-58 St. James's Street ever strayed to the forensic nature of fires and the evidentiary markers at a fire scene.

Pell never mentioned this fact. His survival skills were not very highly developed, but they were developed enough. Indeed, through most of his first team meeting, he did his best to keep his ears open but his mouth shut. The least he could do was pay deference to the professionals—even if, according to Mott, his role was to shake up their conventional way of thinking.

Late in that first meeting, Pell finally decided that he had something worthwhile to contribute. He took a deep breath and plunged ahead. "I would like to talk about the straggler fires," he said.

"What's a 'straggler fire'?" Curtis scowled.

"The ones that ignite after the first wave in any particular neighborhood," said Pell. "What explains this? A second round of deliveries? Or a delay of some kind?"

No one answered. Obviously, no one knew. "What are you driving at, Pell?" Curtis said finally.

"I think it's doubtful that a saboteur would return to the same neighborhood once his initial plan for that neighborhood had succeeded. From the breadth of these fires, it's apparent that no one neighborhood is his objective. Returning, therefore, creates an additional, unnecessary risk that moving on to a new area avoids while accomplishing the same destructive ends."

"Meaning?" MacDonald asked.

"Meaning that, in all likelihood, all of our hypothetical incendiary devices were delivered to one area at one time," Pell continued. "So either some mysterious timing mechanism within the device spaces out the detonations, or some action by the recipient sets the device off. And since conjuring a mysterious timing mechanism, one that then turns to ash, is likely to give me a migraine, I'd first like to test the latter theory: that the recipient, presumably unwittingly, sets the device off."

"Test it how?" asked Dorothy.

"By looking at the straggler fires," said Pell. "If the recipient triggers the fire—by opening the parcel, let's say—one thing that might explain why some fires didn't start until the next night, or the night after, is that the house was empty the day the parcel arrived. Maybe it wasn't opened until a later day because that's the day the resident returned."

Sergeant MacDonald made a note. "It's certainly worth looking into, Mr. Pell," he said. "The straggler fires, and where these people were the day before."

"'These people' are dead, MacDonald," said Curtis.

"Someone may know. Family, business associates, neighbors, even the cop on the beat," MacDonald replied.

"Are you suggesting that these parcels sat on various doorsteps for days on end, even after neighboring houses went up in flames, with no one noticing?" Curtis asked.

"No," said Pell. "Someone would have noticed a parcel

left untouched on the doorstep. That's why I'm suggesting the opposite. If these residents were away until the day their own fires started, then I think the odds are that their parcels waited for them *inside* the house."

"Excuse me?" said Curtis.

"That the parcel was passed through the 'Judas window,'" said Pell.

"Does anyone know what the hell he's talking about? Or is it just me?" Curtis asked.

"It's a window nobody thinks of as a window," Pell explained. "Technically, a 'Judas window' is the device on a prison cell door that lets the guard look in without the prisoner knowing it. A friend of mine wrote a book claiming that every door has a 'Judas window.' You needn't go as far as he did to find a 'Judas window' in the front door of every house in London. After all, how is your post delivered?"

"Through the letter box?" Dorothy suggested.

"Exactly," said Pell. "The mail slot."

"You think the device was able to fit through a letter box?" asked MacDonald.

"I'm suggesting that maybe the device was *designed* to fit through a letter box," Pell replied. "And if I'm right about the straggler fires, I'm willing to strike the 'maybe.'"

"All highly speculative," said Giles Curtis.

"Perhaps so," said Stuart MacDonald, "but if we can verify the bit about the stragglers, Mr. Pell's proposal kicks the ball quite a way down the pitch. Instead of an undefined device, we have some very specific criteria to work with."

"And if he's mistaken, we've wasted precious time chasing phantoms," Curtis replied.

"What's our alternative, Mr. Curtis?" Stuart asked.

"You had a good morning, Mr. Pell," said Dorothy Tanner after the meeting broke.

Pell smiled. "Thank you, Miss Tanner." He'd reached the same conclusion, but liked hearing it from someone else.

"I was just as uncomfortable my first day, not sure when to speak. But I summoned my courage and made what proved to be a significant observation. About the absence of a pattern."

"Ah, yes. That must have been very gratifying."

"It was. Though afterwards, no one said anything. A kind word can go such a long way. I thought you deserved better."

"It's very considerate of you. And you're right about my feeling uncomfortable. Like a missionary sitting with cannibals waiting for dinner to be served."

Dorothy laughed. "Speaking of food," she said, "Sergeant MacDonald asked me to meet him at two o'clock to discuss the best way to go about nailing down the whereabouts of the straggler residents, but I'm free until then. Would you like to join me for lunch?"

"So we may discuss ways to introduce itching powder into Giles Curtis' knickers?" Dorothy tried, without great success, not to react. "What's the matter?" Pell asked.

"I think you mean 'pants,' Mr. Pell. *I* wear knickers. Giles and you, I imagine, wear pants. Under your trousers."

"You never know, Miss Tanner. You never know."

The American Bar, a popular spot for U.S. and Canadian personnel, was in The Stafford, a hotel on St. James's Street near MI5 headquarters. Pell and Dorothy settled down at a small table. He ordered a pint of beer, she a half-pint, and both the fish special.

"I'm a big fan, by the way," Dorothy said. "Read all the Inspector Barnaby books, some more than once. 'Course, I always thought you were one of us. I may have to reevaluate."

"Please do. Do you own copies or are you a library borrower?"

"I borrow, I'm afraid."

"That's too bad—although finding copies to purchase isn't easy these days." Pell took a sip of beer. "So—how did a nice girl like you get into the spook business?"

"I took a wrong turn out of Fortnum & Mason," Dorothy replied. London's premier grocer was located one block up Piccadilly from St. James's Street.

"Isn't that precisely how Giles Curtis landed *his* job?"

It was the last time Curtis' name was mentioned over lunch. Itching powder never came up. Instead, the two discussed subjects ranging from his growing up in America, Claire and the girls, her aging father whom she supported, the

Barnaby novels, his BBC scripts, and the latest war news, including America's entry and the dwindling prospects of a German invasion.

Dorothy was a good listener, better than Mildred. Pell hadn't had someone to talk to this way since his family relocated. The conversation proceeded so naturally that he never once stopped to consider whether this lunch and their prolonged exchange had been requested, perhaps even ordered, by Dorothy's superiors.

If, in fact, Pell was being probed by Dorothy Tanner, there were worse fates. Dorothy was in her late twenties with auburn hair, a pretty face, and trim build. Loneliness was an unavoidable casualty of war, and Pell was not immune from its ravages. He did, however, know and fear the consequences of its cure, and vowed not to succumb.

10. PELL CONSULTS AN EXPERT

Since the 8th of December, Pell's daily routine obviously had changed, and Mildred had started to ask questions.
Most days, Pell already was gone when Mildred arrived, and
did not return before she left. He'd given her a key, so she
could come in, collect and sort the mail, organize the bills,
write checks to pay the ones due, and walk to the bank to deposit Pell's royalties. When Pell returned home, he would find
a neat pile of letters and checks to sign — along with his dread-
ed Christmas cards — that Mildred sealed, stamped, and post-
ed the next morning. Most days, Mildred drank her afternoon
tea alone.

"Research," had been Pell's explanation. "I've been
spending every day at the London Library, researching village
life in the Outer Hebrides in the 18th century." The library was
in St. James's Square, close to MI5, so even a discarded London Transport bus ticket couldn't contradict his cover story.

Mildred knew Pell's aversion to discussing the details
of works in progress, so Pell anticipated no follow-up questions. He was wrong. "Don't you need a notebook, if you're
doing research?" she asked. On the days Pell's and Mildred's
paths crossed, either coming or going, Pell was empty-handed.
"Would you like me to find you one?"

"No need," said Pell. "The library has lockers for rent. I
leave my supplies there. Why lug them back and forth?" Pell
almost was telling the truth. Curtis forbid them from remov-

ing files, papers, and notes from the building.

And Mildred seem satisfied.

Dorothy Tanner and Stuart MacDonald completed their investigation of the fires that started days after the initial blazes in an area. No one knew the movements of many killed by the straggler fires, but enough could be traced to confirm that Pell had been right. These victims weren't home when the fires began. And fires ignited two or three days later often were in homes where the residents had been out of town.

"There were so many victims and so few survivors," Dorothy remarked after she and MacDonald presented their report to the team. "Isn't that odd? All these fires and none without fatalities? None where everybody escaped? One or more deaths in every house? You'd think that by sheer chance, there'd at least be one fire where everyone got out alive."

"That certainly was the case with the Blitz incendiary fires," said Keith Hall. "More often than not, everyone had a fighting chance to escape. If they couldn't put the incendiary out first." During the Blitz, the public received detailed instructions on how to use a stirrup hand pump to douse an incendiary bomb.

"Doesn't that corroborate our theory that the occupant did something to trigger the device?" Pell said. "You can't escape if you're overcome by the initial flash."

"Damn the ARP," said MacDonald, "for removing those bodies. Their locations would tell us definitively."

"Overcome by something so small that it fits through a letter box?" asked Curtis. "That is the current thinking, isn't it?"

"Not small necessarily," said Pell. "After all, the size of the opening constrains only two of an item's three dimensions: width and height. The third dimension — length — isn't affected. There are hunting rifles I could push through a mail slot, if they're thin enough and the stock isn't too wide. Our saboteur still has a lot of room within which to do damage."

"And that assumes the complete device is in one piece," Dorothy added. "It could be in multiple parts — "

" — which ignites when the parts are assembled," Pell continued. "Interesting concept."

Giles Curtis scowled. To the casual observer, he was merely expressing his annoyance that, although the team had made some peripheral progress, it had yet to produce one concrete lead he could report up the chain of command. In truth, his immediate concern was something else. Mott had put both Dorothy Tanner and Anthony Pell on this team over his objections. Now they were completing each other's sentences. Were they working together? A team within the team? Mott's private team within the team? Spook work — catching spies and turning them into double agents — was a natural breeding ground for paranoia, and Giles Curtis had been doing spook work for years.

"We're getting nowhere," he said at last. "Lots of theories. Few facts."

"That's because we don't know anything," Pell replied.

"Speak for yourself," said Giles.

"I'm referring to specific things we need to know, but don't. We're not chemists, we're not experts in triggers, fuses, ignition systems. Even Keith and his boys aren't experts in novel ways to *start* a fire."

Hall, Tomlinson, and Weston nodded their agreement. "I told Chief Firebrace pretty much the same thing when he assigned me to this job," Hall added.

"What do you propose, Pell?" Curtis asked.

"I have a friend, a chemistry professor at the University of London. Alfred French. Used to live on Gower Street in Bloomsbury, near the University."

"Heard from him recently?" asked MacDonald. "Gower Street was where the fires began."

"There's no one named French on the victim list," Dorothy said, looking through her file.

"The University relocated outside London last year. Professor French is alive and well and living in Edinburgh," said Pell. "He's the expert I consult whenever I write about poisons, corrosives, explosives, anything involving chemistry. I propose we talk to him now."

"What's his security clearance?" asked Curtis.

"How should I know?" said Pell.

"How do you propose we consult on a top secret matter with someone who has no security clearance?"

"I'll tell him it's for a book I'm writing. He's used to

that."

"A book about fires starting mysteriously all around London?"

"No, a book about, oh, I don't know—someone trying to destroy secret papers filed in an archive somewhere. He can't get inside the archive, so he finds a way to get the archivist, without realizing what he's doing, to start a fire big enough to destroy everything in the archive—and kill the archivist, so he can't talk about how it happened. And then I say, 'Any ideas, Professor?'"

"Won't he make the connection?" asked Curtis.

"He's been in Scotland for a year. I doubt he reads much about London nightlife."

"Even if his own house nearly bought it?"

"That was two months ago. A lot of other things have happened since."

Giles shook his head. "Mott won't like this. He's even more suspicious of boffins than I am."

"'Boffins'?" Twelve years in Britain and still Pell didn't know all the local lingo.

"Eggheads. Scientists."

"Put the archive someplace specific," said Mott. "Somewhere far from London. What about your National Archives in Washington?"

"Sorry, Colonel, but I'm not writing a book about burning up the Constitution and the Declaration of Independence. I won't even pretend to be writing such a book. Certainly not in wartime. Plus, French knows Inspector Barnaby works here."

"Who's Inspector Barnaby?" Curtis asked.

"Giles, you really must try to read something for the simple pleasure of it," said Mott. "Someplace in Oxford or Cambridge, then," he said turning to Pell. "They have a lot of papers."

"Burn down the Bodleian?" Pell asked. "Isn't that overdoing it?"

"Then a solicitor's office in Leeds," said Mott. "Solicitors keep sensitive papers."

"Solicitors who lock everyone out of their offices attract very few new clients."

"A bank vault, then. They're kept locked."

"Safe deposit boxes are fireproof."

"Pell, you're the writer," said Mott finally. "You come up with something. Just keep it far away from London. The Isle of Man, maybe."

At a few minutes before 10:00 a.m., Pell boarded the Flying Scotsman at King's Cross for the four-hundred-mile, seven-hour journey north. It shouldn't take seven hours, Pell thought, to concoct a decent enough story idea to present to his friend.

The train traveled across the Welland Viaduct connecting Northamptonshire to Rutland, past Peterborough, changed engines at York, continued past Durham Cathedral, over the

River Tyne to Newcastle, across the Royal Border Bridge at Berwick and into Scotland, and on to Edinburgh's Waverly Street station. It arrived only forty minutes late.

He had wired French to meet him at the Café Royal on West Register Street, near the rail station, at six o'clock. Pell had just enough time.

The professor was punctual as always. "Anthony," French called, his hand outstretched to grasp Pell's, while his other hand held a rolled umbrella.

"Hello, Alfred. How are the Scots treating you?"

"As well as anyone is entitled to expect during a war."

"And Elsa?" Pell asked as they sat. Elsa was French's wife.

"Elsa finds Scottish food an abomination." Elsa French was famous in University circles for her gourmet cooking. "The only Scottish dish she finds tolerable, surprisingly enough, is haggis." Haggis is a traditional Scottish dish made by taking chopped sheep organs, mixing them with grain and spices, and boiling the mixture in a sheep's stomach.

"I'll try to remember that," said Pell.

"She says it's the only food with any flavor in the entire country."

Pell went to the bar, returning with two pints of beer. "The University still chugging along?" he asked once he'd sat down again.

"I repeat, as well as anyone is entitled to expect during a war. Not surprisingly, the forces claimed many of my most promising students."

"Which should leave you with more time for your own research."

"I miss my laboratory in London. But enough about me. What brings you to Edinburgh?"

"*My* research," said Pell, although this time it would not be about village life in the Outer Hebrides in the 18th century. "Inspector Barnaby has his first case in Scotland."

"Scotland Yard comes to Scotland. How ironic."

"He's come to investigate a deadly fire in the vault of the Royal Bank of Scotland. The main vault door is opened. Two men enter. They use their two keys to open the little door to a safe deposit box. One man pulls out the box. He hands it to the other. The other opens the box and the whole thing bursts into a fireball destroying the contents of the box and killing its owner. All that's left is ashes, a charred metal box, and a dead body. Is it possible?"

"An explosive triggered when the box is opened? Certainly, it's possible."

"No, not an explosive. A fire."

"Why a fire? Why not an explosive?" French asked.

"Because there's nothing miraculous about a steel box armed with an explosive. A spontaneous, consuming fire has a mysterious, other-worldly quality. Besides, an explosive is sure to kill the guy opening the box. In my story, his death was an accident. You're meant to think it was intended, but it wasn't. It's a misdirection, to divert your suspicion from the dead owner. All he wanted to do was destroy the contents of the box in front of a witness. To absolve himself of responsibility. But he accidentally overcooked the — whatever. The whatever is why I need you. To help me make this possible."

"When were the papers put in the box?"

"You tell me," said Pell. "I can work with whatever works for you."

"Any unusual odor left behind?"

"Magnesium," Pell said reflexively. He hadn't anticipated the question. Maybe he'd said too much.

"Why magnesium?"

"I must have read it somewhere."

"The Germans used magnesium in their incendiary bombs. Magnesium and thermite."

"Maybe that's where I read it," said Pell.

"What if, instead of magnesium, all the paper in the box is treated with nitrocellulose," French said. "What magicians call 'flash paper.' It bursts into flames at the touch of a match. Barnaby would know about flash paper, being a magician and all."

"No doubt."

"Someone switches the documents in the safe deposit box for sheets of flash paper. Then all you need is something rigged inside the box to strike a match when the box opens."

"But flash paper goes 'poof' and is gone," said Pell.

"Like magic. Right up your alley, Anthony."

"It doesn't start a bigger fire."

"It will destroy, or appear to destroy, everything in the safe deposit box." French replied.

"But it won't kill the box's owner," said Pell.

"Do you really need that part?"

"It's essential to my story."

French resisted. "Nitrocellulose is perfect for ninety percent of what you need," he said. "Can't you work around the rest? Find something else that diverts suspicion from the owner."

"No, Alfred. The owner—the guy who opens the box—has to die in the fire."

"Do you really want the 'whodunit' to be a dead man?" French asked. "Won't that weaken your ending?"

"What—now *you're* the mystery writer?"

"It just seems to me that—"

Pell interrupted. "Please, let me worry about the story. All I'm asking you to figure out is: what chemical can create a spontaneous fireball?"

11. Mott Says 'No'

"The entire exercise was ridiculous," Pell told Raymond Mott upon his return from Scotland. "French kept giving me perfectly valid solutions to the problem I gave him, but none fit the problem we really have. And I couldn't edge closer to the problem we really have without running afoul of your security concerns." Giles Curtis barely hid his glee.

"It was always an improbability," Mott said.

"Only because I couldn't level with him."

"That's what it means to keep official secrets."

"And that rubbish about the *Bismark* and 'I don't care how you do it'?" Pell shot back. "What was that all about?"

"Pell, half the boffins in England have German colleagues. They're all intermarried, academically speaking. Not one of them can be trusted."

Pell was unconvinced. "The Royal Family married Germans. You trust them, don't you?"

"A few. But quite a number of that lot I'd throw into Wormwood Scrubs if I could have my way."

"I've known Alfred French for nine years. Damn it, his own house was fifty feet from burning to the ground."

"No," said Mott.

"Then find me someone else. Otherwise, we're never going to get anywhere."

"What's crawling under your skin?" Dorothy asked

Pell as they left the building.

"I don't know what I'm doing here," Pell replied. "Every contribution I offer, either Giles mocks or Mott shoots down."

"Giles Curtis is a wanker, but don't quote me. Raymond Mott, on the other hand, is a decent chap."

"Decent more properly describes the size of the stick he's got up his—"

"Now, now, Mr. Pell," she rushed to interject. "Plus, you're not being fair. Mott doesn't shoot down all your ideas. He agreed to the enhanced police patrols and BBC warnings, didn't he?"

"He had no other choice. It was the safe, by-the-book decision. Anything else would have put him at enormous risk if something preventable then happened."

"And it stopped the fires, thanks to you," she said.

"That doesn't help us catch and question the saboteur," Pell replied. "Isn't that the mission?"

"It gives us time to catch and question the saboteur."

"You're missing the larger point, Dorothy. Mott persuaded me to join your merry band with a big song and dance about how essential I was because I think differently. How all of you learned from the same book while I write my own. Yet when push comes to shove, he goes by your worn, yellowing book every time."

"He won't let you consult your professor friend?"

"Worse. He *will* let me consult my friend as long as I

don't say anything to make the consultation useful."

"For security reasons," she presumed.

"For security reasons. The hush-hush 'Silent Blitz.' Lord Beaverbook must have missed the meeting."

"The fires aren't the secret. *We* are. Our findings, our conclusions, our theories."

"Theories which will remain theories, unproven and unprovable, unless we find someone we trust with the knowledge necessary to complete the picture. I trust Alfred French. Raymond Mott doesn't, because Raymond Mott doesn't know him, let alone know him as well as I do."

"Anthony, please believe me when I tell you this: Colonel Mott knows a lot more about a lot of people than even their closest family and friends know. He won't talk about what he knows, but don't for a minute assume he's shooting in the dark."

Bruno Danziger was growing restless. Every week he returned to London anticipating a message relayed from Germany. Whatever its form, the communication required extreme care to minimize the obvious dangers. But Danziger was told to expect a message nonetheless.

His instructions were clear: initiate no further contact; he will be notified what to do next. Meanwhile, maintain his regular routine in order to ensure receipt when the time came —and wait.

***

Dorothy's words were a recurring distraction for Pell. "Colonel Mott knows a lot more about a lot of people than even their closest family and friends know." Pell's imagination—his mystery writer's imagination—shifted naturally into gear. Is everyone looking at these puzzle pieces the wrong way around, he wondered. Is this a human example of the old *Puck* cartoon, depicting either a young girl or an old lady depending how you looked at it?

What, thought Pell, if Mott didn't recruit me for the reasons he gave? What if Alfred French has been his target all along? For the "Silent Blitz" fires, or for something else? And, already knowing our relationship, Mott is using me to get to Alfred? Has MI5 been following us both for months?

The more he thought, the less sense it made. The whole task force can't be a subterfuge, a pretext designed entirely to cause Pell to want to meet with French. That's ridiculous. What if Pearl Harbor had never happened? What if Pell had never agreed to participate? If Mott were investigating French, there were more direct, more effective means at his disposal. This elaborate dog-and-pony show wouldn't be necessary, and certainly wasn't worth the exceedingly remote chance that it would prompt Pell to lead Mott to Alfred French.

And yet, Pell wanted to be sure.

Pell let a few days pass. He then found the ideal reason to seek a private audience with Colonel Mott.

"How may I be of service?" Mott began.

"When we spoke about my friend Alfred French the

other day, were you entirely candid with me?"

"In what regard?"

"Has Alfred come under direct suspicion for any reason? You spoke about British scientists in general, but later I had cause to wonder whether you were being deliberately vague. That you may know something negative about Alfred that I don't."

"'Cause,' you say. What 'cause'? What made you wonder, as you put it, about my suspicions?"

"Just a figure of speech," Pell replied.

"Nothing is ever just a figure of speech. Either *you* came into possession of some information that made even you suspicious of French—"

"No, nothing of the kind," Pell replied immediately.

"—or someone apprised you of the fact that I often know, but will not discuss, reliable information of a suspicious nature about certain people."

Pell considered Mott's last statement for a brief moment and then smiled. "Dorothy spoke to you, didn't she?"

"Dorothy Tanner is my eyes and ears on your team. I trust her, not because she is especially trustworthy—although she may be—but because everyone else is far less trustworthy. Starting with Giles Curtis, a duplicitous tosser if ever there was one."

"You noticed."

"I'm not a complete idiot. Even Austen's Mr. Woodhouse would have noticed," said Mott. "Or don't you read

Emma in the States?"

"Woodhouse, the chump. Yes, Colonel, I get the reference. But at the moment, sir, what I am noticing most is your deft avoidance of my original question."

"Then let me answer your original question with a question of my own: If I do collect such information, but as a rule do not discuss it with my staff; and if I do possess such information about Professor French, what makes you think I would tell you about it?"

Pell reached into his pocket and withdrew a folded telegram. Unfolding and laying it before Mott, he said, "This is why. It's a wire I received from Alfred early this morning."

Mott looked down. The telegram read: "IS YOUR SUDDEN INTEREST IN SPONTANEOUS COMBUSTION INSPIRED BY THE RECENT RASH OF APPARENTLY SPONTANEOUS LONDON FIRES"

"What did you say to him?" Mott asked, his eyes locked on Pell's.

"Nothing. I swear. Documents in a safe deposit box, and the owner of that box, in the vault of the Royal Bank of Scotland. That's all we discussed. Although I may have mentioned something about magnesium."

"Why would you do that?"

"Because he asked about odors, and I wanted an answer in the general vicinity of our problem."

Mott considered the situation carefully. "He must know your mind very well," he said finally. "I'm struck by his word 'inspired.' As if he knows how you get your ideas. Do many of your ideas spring from actual events?"

"Ideas spring from pretty much everything."

"Is your inspiration a subject you and French have discussed?"

"I told you—"

"I don't mean on this last visit. In the past."

Pell searched his memory. "It's possible. I don't remember specifically," he said.

"Perhaps that's all this means. Not that I will presume that's all this means." With practiced ease, Mott slid open his center oak desk drawer with his left hand while simultaneously slipping French's wire into the drawer with his right.

"Colonel," said Pell, growing impatient, "do you suspect Alfred French?"

Mott grinned. "I do now," he said.

12. THE CONSPIRATORS

"I know now not to confide anything in you," Pell said the next time he saw Dorothy Tanner.

"I didn't tell Mott anything you said to me in confidence," Dorothy replied. "In fact, what I said to him was more *what I told you* than what you told me."

"Really? And why did you tell me what you told me?"

"So you might give Mott's decision more deference."

"Well, when you repeated what you said to me, you essentially told Mott that I'd complained to you about him."

"You didn't complain so much as express frustration, doubting the value of your contribution," Dorothy said.

"Is that what you told him? That I was pouting?"

"No, that you want to do everything possible to solve this case."

Pell paused. "Dorothy, when you told Mott what you told me—that Mott perhaps knew something about Alfred French that I didn't know—how did he react?"

"He listened."

"Did he smile? Did he look surprised? Was he annoyed that you'd said what you said?"

"He just listened. Mott's quite accustomed to keeping his cards close to his vest."

"We've got to get a peek at those cards," Pell said.

"Excuse me?"

"I have to know what Mott knows. Whether I'm wrong

to trust French."

"Where you're wrong is in distrusting Colonel Mott."

"Aren't you a whiz at the MI5 filing system?"

"Don't remind me," Dorothy answered.

"Does Mott have private files?"

"No comment."

"Come on, Dorothy."

"I will not help you steal MI5 files, Anthony."

"Not steal. Read."

"Most of these files are top secret."

"Most but not all. I can't know if this one is before I look at it. Besides, there may be no file. You can't get in trouble for not reading a non-existent file."

"No, Anthony, I will not join your little conspiracy. I have a delicate neck that chafes when a rope is placed around it."

"Coward."

"You'll have to find another way."

Home Secretary Herbert Morrison contemplated rattling Raymond Mott's cage to provoke accelerated action in the London fire investigation, but doubted it would do much good. Mott was not one to take his responsibilities lightly. If progress was slow, there must be a good reason. Besides, the fires had stopped, as had the sensational press coverage.

In truth, Morrison's only reason to stir the pot was in case the PM raised the issue, so he could report his personal effort to compel an expeditious result. But even this justification was now moot. Morrison was privy to top secret information that, at this moment, Winston Churchill was aboard the battleship *HMS Duke of York* en route to Washington, D.C. via Norfolk, Virginia. Soon the PM would be forming a worldwide war strategy with President Roosevelt. The London fires were the least of his concerns.

The Home Secretary opted to leave Mott's cage alone.

"Colonel?"

"Yes, Pell."

"My telegram from Professor French that you brushed into your top drawer?"

"What about it?"

"Is it wise for us not to answer Alfred's wire?" Pell asked. He thought the "us" was a nice touch.

"How would you propose to respond?" Mott answered another question with a question.

"I'm not sure, Colonel. There may be things I don't know that I might inadvertently give away." It was Pell's turn to shoot in the dark. Then again, thought Pell, Mott must recognize this as a legitimate concern if, indeed, MI5 had gathered specific intelligence on Professor Alfred French.

"I appreciate your caution," Mott replied. "Putting that consideration aside, what would be your most natural response?"

"Something like: 'I guess the "Silent Blitz" isn't so

silent where the subconscious is concerned.' It's simple, gives nothing away, substitutes humor for evasion, and in a sense, answers his question."

"Pell, for a foreigner, you have quite a flair for the English language."

"My years in Britain apparently did wonders for me."

"I like your approach," said Mott. "Go ahead. Send it."

Pell left Mott's office convinced he now had his answer about Mott's knowledge of Alfred French. Mott never would have been so casual about a formal communication with someone he suspected of disloyalty. If French was someone in whom Mott had taken a special interest, Mott would have wired back already, in Pell's name — and in a manner likely to provoke a further response. He wouldn't have waited for Pell to suggest an answer. Furthermore, Pell's proposed language was a conversation-ender, not designed to prompt French to do anything. Everything about this exchange was inconsistent with Dorothy's theory, Mott's caginess on the subject aside.

Pell was relieved.

Professor French contemplated the curious biography of his brilliant graduate student, twenty-six-year-old Bruno Danziger. Danziger was born in Germany, emigrated to Great Britain four years ago, lived alone in East London, and gave every appearance of becoming an exceptional chemist. He had not been interned as an enemy alien upon the outbreak of hostilities, was not yet eligible for British citizenship, and had never been conscripted into military service for reasons French never learned. Danziger did not discuss his private life, politics, or the war. He was an enigma in every respect other than his academic work.

For these reasons, when Alfred French received Anthony Pell's wire mentioning the "Silent Blitz," French's thoughts turned immediately to Bruno Danziger.

13. Preparing to Resume

Despite their pyrotechnic lull, The Bat remained hard at work. Night after night, alone in the dark. The Postman and The Bat foresaw Berlin soon demanding a new rash of fires, wider in area but more compressed in time. A sufficient number of devices for such an intense onslaught had to be built in advance. There wouldn't be enough time between attacks for The Bat to manufacture them delivery run by delivery run.

The Postman was useless at this part. He was useless in the blackness. His moment for frenetic activity would come soon enough. Deliveries would have to be made at an unprecedented pace.

The men knew their luck couldn't hold out indefinitely. Their best chance of success was an all out lightning strike — a true blitzkrieg.

But when? What timing would maximize the disruption of life on the British home front? The answer was obvious.

Christmas was coming.

14. LIGHTNING STRIKES

On the night of Monday, 22 December, the fires began again — this time in Kensington.

"These barmpots were warned repeatedly not to open unexpected parcels," Stuart MacDonald said when the team met early the next morning. "What's coming through the letter box that's so irresistible, Bank of England money sacks?"

"Thursday is Christmas," said Dorothy. "People expect parcels."

"Which likely explains why our saboteur picked this week to resurface," Pell added.

"ARP has not removed any of the bodies," Keith Hall reported. "Tomlinson, Weston, and I are headed out this morning to take photographs."

"Accompanied by a forensic team from the Yard," said MacDonald.

"When will we get their findings?" Curtis asked.

"They're briefing me at two. Hall and I can brief the team at three o'clock," MacDonald answered.

The meeting stood adjourned.

"Let's have it," said Giles Curtis when the task force reconvened at 3:00 p.m.

"It's interesting," said MacDonald. "All those bodies burned beyond recognition? All sitting or lying down at the time. At least it looks that way. The chair, the sofa, the bed —

whichever furniture they may have been sitting or lying on —
also burned intensely. They were found on top of that furniture. They could have fallen on top of the furniture, but more
likely, they were sitting or lying down at the time."

"Which means what?" Curtis asked.

"Which means we have a pattern," said Pell. "That elusive but ever enlightening phenomenon, the pattern."

MacDonald elaborated. "It also means — presuming
we're going with the parcel theory — that they sat down, or lay
down, opened the parcel, and triggered an ignition so intense
that they were instantly brown bread."

"Or —," said Pell.

"Or what?" said Curtis.

"Or they were asleep when the fire struck," said Pell.
"The parcel emitted a chemical that made them tired, caused
them to sit or lie down, and after it put them to sleep, it burst
into flames when they were helpless to escape."

"Seems a bit far-fetched, don't you think?" said Curtis.

"It would answer one question," Dorothy Tanner said.
"The last post is delivered at around two o'clock in the afternoon. The majority of the fires start at night. Why the delay?
We said it's because the fires don't start until the parcel is
opened. Then why don't they start at six o'clock, when people
get home from work? Something else delays the ignition. Mr.
Pell's idea is as good as any."

"Miss Tanner," said Giles Curtis, "I have the sneaking
suspicion that you would agree with Mr. Pell if he proposed

that Father Christmas delivered the incendiary devices."

"Only if all the fires started Christmas Eve," said Pell. "If they all started Christmas morning, we'd look for parcels marked 'Do not open until Christmas.' Hey, maybe each one said: 'Do not open until 9:00 p.m.'"

"This is a serious business, Pell," Curtis barked.

"Don't tell *me* that, Curtis. A serious business is handled by serious people. When it involves questions of chemistry, serious chemistry people must be consulted."

"That's between you and Mott," Curtis replied. "Let's move on, shall we?"

"How can we move on? We're still stuck in the mud. We have no chemistry expert, no arson expert. We have nothing but coppers, firemen, and spooks."

"Plus one file clerk and one teller of tall tales," said Curtis.

"And you, Giles, an officious, pig-headed lout."

"Do you feel better?" Dorothy asked Pell when they finally were alone. "I hope you feel better, because you certainly didn't accomplish anything else."

"A fire that initially bursts into a massive conflagration has different chemical properties than a chemical reaction that emits a slow, steady stream of, say, carbon monoxide, disabling a person, before graduating to the burned-beyond-recognition stage."

"We've been through this before."

"Mott doesn't know anything about Alfred French other than that he is a British scientist, which automatically makes him a suspected fifth columnist in Mott's eyes."

"How to you know that?" Dorothy asked.

"Because he practically told me," said Pell. "Not in so many words, but the implication was clear. I also told him, okay, you don't like Alfred, find me somebody else. And he hasn't—because to Raymond Mott, they're all not to be trusted. I've about had it with government service."

"In wartime, you don't get to pick and choose."

"If Uncle Sam wants me, I'm his. In this business, however, I'm a day laborer and my labor is done."

"Anthony, please don't take that attitude. I know these people better than you do. Mott will call the Home Secretary, the Home Secretary will speak to the Prime Minister, the Prime Minister will cable President Roosevelt, and in forty-eight hours, you will be Private Anthony Pell, United States Army, assigned to MI5 at the King's pleasure."

"Isn't there something in the Magna Carta—?"

"No." She paused. "I don't want to see you hurt."

"I know. Thank you."

They walked out onto St. James's Street in the crisp December air. "Where are you spending Christmas?" she asked. "In Cambridge with Claire's family?"

"No, they're visiting friends in Cumbria. I'm not a big holiday person. I'll listen to some carols on the radio—the wireless—reread a little Dickens, eat whatever's in the fridge."

"Why don't you spend Christmas with me and my Dad? His body's not very agile, but his mind's still as sharp as a razor. And he's awfully sweet. He worked for the Great Western Railway for forty years. He was a wheeltapper."

"What's that?"

"I'll let him tell you. It's fascinating. He has lots of marvelous stories. And he loves your books. Please come."

"How could I resist?"

"That's the spirit."

"Don't complain to me, Giles," Mott said, "Use some leadership skills."

"Bloody Yank. They're all cowards, waiting for a war to practically be won before showing up for the fight."

"True, but then again, they have less to do with starting the fight than we do."

"And it's not just Pell," said Curtis. "He and that Tanner woman are as thick as thieves."

"Dorothy Tanner is a loyal member of MI5. She's been especially helpful working on Mr. Pell. Helping to make him more of a team player."

"If that's what she's trying to do," Curtis replied, "she's made a total cock-up of it."

The Kensington fires continued igniting Tuesday afternoon and evening—the 23rd of December. Unlike in the past, however, an overlapping rash of fires also broke out in Mayfair Tuesday night into Wednesday—*before* the Kensington fires had run their course. The "Silent Blitz" not only was back, it was intensifying.

15. PELL'S CHRISTMAS

Keith Hall, Leonard Tomlinson, and Bennett Weston were almost too exhausted to drag themselves into work at 57-58 St. James's Street on the morning of Wednesday, 24 December. The three had spent the whole of Tuesday night fighting fires in both Kensington and Mayfair. Experienced firemen were at a premium Tuesday night and so, seconded to MI5 or not, Hall, Tomlinson, and Weston were summoned to don fire helmets and join a crew.

"All of my reports on last night's fires are consistent with what we witnessed from the night before," said Hall. "Victims found burned to a crisp in a chair, on a sofa, in a bed, or the reasonable approximation of these positions."

"But," said Stuart MacDonald with great emphasis, and then repeated the word so that his emphasis could not be missed, "but—this was not true of the straggler fires in Kensington yesterday afternoon and early evening. The victims of these fires died in a wide variety of locations throughout their homes. Some near no furniture at all."

"Meaning they were standing?" Curtis asked.

"Or lying on the floor."

"If they were standing, that would shoot Mr. Pell's soporific theory all to hell, correct?" said Curtis with a grin.

"Unless, as Stuart told you, they first dropped to the floor," Pell replied.

"To sleep, or to avoid the fire?" Hall asked.

"Could be either, I suppose," said MacDonald.

"Aren't we missing the most significant aspect of Stuart and Keith's findings?" Pell said. "It's the pattern of nighttime conduct versus the randomness of daytime conduct. What explains this?"

"If opening the parcel triggers the fire, then most people open the parcel at night, and are sitting or lying down when they do," said Dorothy. "Those who do not open the parcel at night do so any which way."

"But why?" Pell asked.

The meeting broke for lunch with no further progress having been achieved. The American Bar in The Stafford was serving a special pre-Christmas lunch, and Pell convinced Dorothy to give American Christmas dishes a go.

"If I can drink a snowball," he said, referring to the British seasonal drink mixing a custard-like brandy with lemonade, "you can try eggnog. And if you're going to force me to wear a ridiculous paper crown tomorrow, you can eat delicious sweet potato pie today."

Lunch ran late, and it was past three o'clock when Pell and Dorothy returned to work. Everyone Pell passed fell silent, something he failed to notice at first, then mentally brushed aside, and finally could not ignore.

"What's the matter?" he asked.

"Mott wants to see you," was all anyone would say.

Pell rushed to Mott's office and was ushered inside without being announced.

"What's going on?" Pell wanted to know.

"Sit down, Mr. Pell," Mott insisted.

"Has anything happened to Claire or the girls?"

"No. It's your home. It's on fire."

At first, Pell perceived no connection between this fire and any other. Maida Vale had not been a target. It was the middle of the day. He didn't get parcels as a rule. And then came the second bombshell.

"ARP workers found the body of a woman."

"Mildred?" Pell asked. "My secretary is a woman named Mildred Tate. Sixtyish, unmarried, about five-two."

"She was found sitting at a desk, or what's left of it."

"In the first room off the hall to the right?"

"I don't know," said Mott.

"Can I see her?" Pell asked.

"I wouldn't advise it, but someone has to try to make an identification. Does she have any family?"

"Not in Britain. She has a brother who moved to New Zealand years ago."

Pell's mind kept churning, with each thought piling on the next. "Was I the target?" he asked. "For my work here?"

"Who knew of your work here?"

"No one. Not even Mildred. Not even Claire."

"Professor French?"

"Absolutely not. I resent that. I never told Alfred any-thing you and I hadn't agreed upon. Why don't you ask Giles Curtis whom he told I'm now working here?"

Pell's small house in Maida Vale was a total loss. He then went to the morgue to identify Mildred. From her shape under the white sheet, he knew it was her.

Mott was right. Pell shouldn't have looked. Mildred's face was gone, as were her hands. The rest of her body was burned almost as thoroughly. He hoped her death had been quick and painless, but doubted it.

Dorothy waited for him, first outside the morgue room door and then outside the mortuary loo—into which Pell stag-gered and spasmodically relinquished his pre-Christmas American lunch. "Come home with me," she said after he emerged and confirmed he'd regained control of himself. "We have a spare room."

"Shouldn't you check with your father first?" Pell asked. "Before inviting a man to stay over?"

"Before inviting a new audience for his old stories, you mean. Trust me, he'll love it."

It was not a very festive Christmas Eve. Dorothy tried her best to lighten the mood. Mr. Tanner—"William," he in-sisted—also tried, diverting the conversation away from the events of the day whenever possible. So it was that Pell learned, before retiring early to write a long letter to Claire, that a "wheeltapper" is the skilled railroad worker who tests the integrity of each wheel on a train by tapping it with a long-handled hammer and listening for the tone his tap produces. A tap on a sound wheel produces a different tone than a tap on a damaged wheel. The wheeltapper's experienced ear is the sole judge of each wheel's soundness.

At eight o'clock Christmas morning, the Tanners' telephone rang. Dorothy answered it. "Yes, Colonel, I'll tell him," was all she said before hanging up the receiver.

"What else?" Pell asked.

"There were 22 other fires in Maida Vale last night. The Colonel wanted you to know that you may not have been the target after all."

"How did he know I was here?"

"I asked him if it was all right that I invite you over today," she said. "I didn't want either of us to ruffle any feathers should it get out. I doubt he knows you spent the night. Then again, who knows what Raymond Mott knows."

Christmas dinner was the best the Tanners' ration books could provide: mock duck, a concoction made of practically meatless sausages, apples, onions and sage; parsley and celery stuffing; potato floddies made by mixing grated potatoes with some flour and herbs and frying the mixture in a pan; and a makeshift plum pudding made of breadcrumbs with a touch of fruit.

Pell even wore the paper crown with equanimity.

After dinner, William invited Pell to go through his

closet and pick any clothes he wanted to borrow. "I've got more than I'll ever need," he said. "My dancehall days are far behind me."

The three sat together in the front room to listen to the King's Christmas message on the BBC. William then went to bed, leaving his daughter alone with her American colleague.

"He trusts you," she explained. "And he knows me."

"My letter to Claire has one conspicuous omission. I don't think she would understand. Several very respectable London hotels survived the Blitz, and she knows it."

"You're free to go at any time."

But Pell did not want to be alone. Not now. Not after yesterday. He desperately needed something—or someone—to distract him from thoughts of Mildred, and the further trauma of losing his second home in less than a year. He was the only "Silent Blitz" team member, as far as he knew, affected directly by the "Silent Blitz." In other words, were he to demand permission to spring the saboteur's gallows trap door personally, no one on their team could claim priority.

"Shouldn't we check in at some point?" Dorothy asked finally. "To find out what's been going on?"

"Straggler fires in Kensington, Mayfair, and Maida Vale," Pell offered. "No new outbreaks."

"Was there a news bulletin tucked inside your Christmas cracker?" she asked.

"It has to be. Just like there will be no new fires tomorrow. Just like we've never had new fires on a Sunday. What do

Christmas, Boxing Day, and Sundays have in common?"

"No Royal Mail delivery," said Dorothy.

"Exactly. Our guy would never take the risk of delivering his devices on a postal holiday."

Pell telephoned Keith Hall and suggested that Hall pass Pell's forecast up the NFS chain: "Boxing Day will be quiet during the day. But prepare for more fires in Mayfair and Maida Vale tomorrow night, as people return home from spending the holidays away, and find a Christmas Eve parcel inside the door. And then expect a new rash somewhere else on Saturday."

Pell and the Tanners also spent Boxing Day quietly. At 3:00 p.m., the BBC broadcast an original radio thriller, "The Key," by British crime writer Peter Cheyney. Pell and Cheyney were polar opposites in British mystery-writing circles. Pell was an American who wrote in the British "puzzle mystery" style; Cheyney was a Londoner writing in the American "hard-boiled" style made famous by Dashiell Hammett and Raymond Chandler.

The Cheyney play was followed by a 90-minute radio adaptation of J.M. Barrie's *Peter Pan*. As Pell sat engrossed before the Tanners' wireless, he managed to forget the sight of Mildred lying on the morgue table for entire minutes at a time.

Boxing Day was not a quiet one for Raymond Mott. He owed something to Anthony Pell and was determined to provide it at the earliest opportunity.

In the morning, Mott paid a visit to the Home Secretary. "Our task force needs someone with specific expertise investigating fire scenes," Mott said in a tone that permitted no rebuttal.

"Is there such an expert?" Morrison asked.

"Not in London. He's elsewhere in the Empire."

"Where?"

"Canada," Mott replied.

Mott had spoken at length with the NFS Chief of Fire Staff Aylmer Firebrace. He'd also spoken to MI6 and Scotland Yard. Each knew only one person who fit Mott's needs.

"Who is that?" asked the Home Secretary.

"Harry Rethoret," Mott announced. "He's a Canadian insurance investigator working out of Montreal."

"Not someone in government service?"

"No, a private citizen." Morrison looked away as he drummed the fingers of his right hand on the arm of his chair. "Is that a problem?" Mott asked.

"It would be easier if it were an inter-government matter. We have official channels for that at the civil service level. But commandeering a Canadian private citizen requires the intervention of a higher authority. Ordinarily, I would impose upon the PM to make an urgent request of Prime Minister King." Mackenzie King was Prime Minister of Canada.

Mott understood. Ordinarily, Churchill was on British soil, readily available to the Home Secretary. At the moment, however, the Prime Minister was solidifying the Anglo-American alliance with a headline-grabbing visit to President Roosevelt in Washington, D.C. He and FDR held a joint press conference, together lit the White House Christmas tree, and later on Boxing Day, Churchill was addressing a joint session of the U.S. Congress.

"Ottawa is a less expensive telephone call from Washington than it is from London," Mott offered.

"Winston won't appreciate the interruption."

"He will when Mr. Roosevelt insists on showing him the famous stamp collection. He'll welcome any reason to excuse himself."

"John Martin is staying in the White House with the PM," Morrison said. Martin was Churchill's Principal Private Secretary. "But I don't believe Elizabeth made the trip." Elizabeth Layton was the Prime Minister's personal secretary. "She can send a secure cable to Martin explaining why the PM should place a call to Prime Minister King."

The Home Secretary was not eager to remind the PM of Mott's lingering, unresolved investigation, but Mott's plea left him no reasonable alternative. For Mott, this was not the optimal way to convey an urgent request, but Morrison explained that Churchill might be in Washington for several more weeks. Mott couldn't afford to wait.

Morrison and Mott hailed a taxi and headed to 10 Downing Street to put the Home Secretary's plan into motion. Upon arrival, Morrison located Churchill's secretary, explained what he needed, and dictated to Miss Layton the cable to be sent securely to John Martin:

> MOTT SABOTAGE INVESTIGATION RE-
> QUIRES IMMEDIATE ASSISTANCE OF CIVIL-
> IAN MONTREAL FIRE SCENE EXPERT HAR-
> RY RETHORET URGE PM TO CALL PM KING
> TO ARRANGE SECRET AIR TRANSPORT TO
> LONDON MORRISON

Pell was right about no profusion of new fires on Christmas Day or Boxing Day. He did not predict that the literal "ceasefire" would continue the next day as well: Saturday, 27 December.

"Maybe this has nothing to do with the Royal Mail," said Dorothy.

"Too many people were home today. He likes to deliver his parcels to an empty house," Pell replied.

Whether Pell's reasoning was right or wrong, the "Silent Blitz" resumed in Richmond promptly on Monday.

16. RETHORET IN LONDON

Harry Rethoret flew from Montreal to London on a Lancaster bomber converted to civil use by Trans-Canada Air Lines, stopping once for refueling in Reykjavik, Iceland. The flight took 12 hours and 26 minutes. Company Officer Hall met Rethoret at Croydon Airport in South London and drove him back to MI5 headquarters.

Meanwhile, Mott briefed Pell on all that had happened since last they spoke. "You have your expert," Mott said. For the first time in weeks, Pell felt the team might be equal to the task.

As instructed, Hall brought Rethoret directly to Colonel Mott's office. "Welcome to London, Mr. Rethoret," said Mott, greeting his guest. "My apologies for how unceremoniously you were brought here. Secrecy is paramount, and the fewer who knew you were leaving Canada, the better. Is this your first visit?"

"Yes, it is."

"You know why you're here, I presume?"

"I was told someone is starting a lot of fires."

"We suspect German sabotage. The Prime Minister created a special task force under my direction to investigate these fires. Company Officer Hall and his team have been seconded to MI5 for this purpose. A Scotland Yard Special Branch officer and my own personnel are working with them. Special Branch and MI5 are quite experienced in tracking and capturing saboteurs."

"I see."

"Company Officer Hall has the details of each fire and the photographs his team took. I suggest you get started."

"Lesson one about fires," Harry Rethoret told the members of the "Silent Blitz" task force. "Draw the outline of a house on a piece of paper. Pick one spot in the house as the point of origin. Then turn the paper upside down. Imagine water gushing into the upside-down house from the point of origin you selected. The water first cascades down to cover the upside-down ceiling. Then it spreads out laterally, then seeps through to the floors below—that is, above—then out windows, et cetera, et cetera.

"Fires are upside-down floods. Fires move up just like water moves down, although fire burns through walls and ceilings faster than water seeps through."

Rethoret was giving the team a crash course in fire scene investigation. It's about time, thought Pell.

"Fires need three things. Fuel, heat, and oxygen. We call fuel the fire load. No fire load, meaning nothing to burn, and it won't be much of a fire.

"Fires start in one of five ways. Natural, like lightning strikes. Mechanical, like sparks from an engine. Electrical, which you can determine from the condition of the wiring. Accidental, which, by definition, cannot occur in a designed pattern. And incendiary: set on purpose. Generally, you determine that a fire is incendiary either by eliminating the other four possibilities, or by finding evidence of an accelerant. Accelerants leave tell-tale burn marks and chemical residue. This requires taking samples from the various scenes, which will be our first order of business."

The NFS team—Keith Hall, Leonard Tomlinson, and Bennett Weston—revisited all of the fire scenes with Harry Rethoret to collect the samples Rethoret needed to examine. The Canadian pointed to the pieces of charred wood he wanted photographed, bagged, and labeled. The team cut away sections of intensely burnt flooring, and moldings bearing distinctive char marks resembling the skin of an alligator. Wall plaster was demolished so that the electrical wiring near the points of origin could be collected. The team also took samples of the glass it found.

"You can still smell it," said Tomlinson.

"I know," said Hall.

"What's that?" Rethoret asked.

"The smell of magnesium," said Hall.

"Always look to see in which direction the wood is carbonized. In other words, turned into charcoal. Compare the depth of carbonization from place to place. The deeper the carbonization, the closer to the point of origin. Always remember that superheated gases spread upwards. They spread in a V shape. Find the point of the V and you've found the point of origin. And the narrower the V, the hotter the fire."

The team was back at MI5 headquarters, and Rethoret was giving another lesson, this time using the evidence from the various premises to illustrate his points. As he spoke, he marked photographs and diagrams of the scenes to show the points of origin and burn patterns.

"If, however, the shape of the fire is more a U than a V, that means that we don't have a *point* of origin, but what we call a 'pool of origin,' as if someone poured a pool of gasoline — petrol — on the floor. I'm not seeing this anywhere here.

"We do have some 'chimney effect' examples," he said, again marking the photographs. "That's where a very intense fire burns straight up, like it's in its own chimney. It burns through the ceiling before burning the walls, placing the point of origin directly below.

"These were all very intense fires. Look at this glass, the odd cracking patterns. In an intense fire, glass will crack instead of melt. And intense fires generally mean an accelerant was used.

"However, I've found no evidence of an accelerant. There are no traces of a petroleum, kerosene, or other chemical residue at the point of origin. It can burn away, but when there is an accelerant on the floor, on the carpet, on the furniture, usually traces will be left behind."

"Have you reached any conclusions?" Pell asked.

"Preliminarily, each scene has a distinct point of origin, a place of very intense burning — although I don't yet know why. The intensity of the fires is consistent with the use of an accelerant—although I don't yet know what. And for fire scenes where we know the location of the deceased, that location is consistent with the point of origin of the fire."

"Consistent with the victim somehow triggering the ignition of the fire?" asked Pell.

"Maybe, but that would be unusual," said Rethoret. "People don't stand over a fire waiting to be consumed. They move away. Even if they're burning, even if running will only make things worse, they run anyway. You find human remains where devices explode, not where fires start."

"There were no explosions," said Hall.

"But you said these fires were intense," said Pell.

"Correct," said Rethoret.

"A sudden burst of flame, perhaps? A fireball?"

"With the proper chemical agent, that's possible."

"Igniting one's hair, one's clothing, *before* a person could react?"

"That's also unusual. Ignition would have to occur inches from someone's face for something like that to happen."

Pell thought immediately of how Mildred Tate looked under the white sheet on the steel morgue table—her face completely burned away.

17. SPINNING IN CIRCLES

Pell spent the morning planning Mildred's funeral, which would not take place for another three days due to the laws of supply and demand. He asked Mildred's landlord to unlock her small Camden Town flat for him, and found her address book on the kitchen counter. He sent her brother in New Zealand a cable breaking the news and expressing his condolences. Pell also sent a wire to each name he found with a Greater London address about the forthcoming funeral service at St. Michael's Church on Camden Road.

He was still living with the Tanners. He had broached moving to a hotel, but Dorothy scoffed at the idea and her father agreed with his daughter. Officially, Pell remained uncommitted, except that he did notify the Royal Mail to forward his post to the Tanners' home address. When Dorothy saw Pell's letters on the front doormat, under the letter box, she ribbed her boarder mercilessly.

"We get five shillings a week," she said. "Paid in advance." Pell wasn't sure whether to take her seriously. "Too much?" she added. "It's the same price as one three-course dinner at the Ritz. A full week here must be worth one fancy dinner."

"The Ritz would charge more if they could," Pell said. The government had capped hotel meals at five shillings to prevent hotels from exploiting their rations exemption.

"So would we," Dorothy shot back.

The day after Boxing Day, Pell also realized that his clothing ration coupons survived the fire—because, on the morning of Christmas Eve, he had shoved his ration book into his pocket, intending to buy Dorothy a Christmas gift to give her the following day. The fire disrupted his plans, but at least now he could buy enough new clothing to return what he'd borrowed from William.

Dorothy and he began traveling to and from work together. He was certain their joint comings and goings were attracting notice and, while he didn't care for himself, he was concerned that the chatter might affect Dorothy's future. But she dismissed his worry with five words: "They can all sod off." Only one MI5 person's opinion mattered to her, and she knew Raymond Mott cared bugger-all about her friendship with Pell.

During one of the trips from home to work, Pell expressed his reservations about Harry Rethoret's contribution to the team.

"He knows a lot more about fire scenes than we do," Pell admitted, "and obviously is very meticulous, but he's lost on the accelerant question. Some of his findings say yes, others say no, and none say which one. I don't blame him. He doesn't know enough about chemistry to imagine what combination of chemicals explains what happened. Meanwhile, we keep spinning our wheels, getting nowhere."

"Rethoret is considered the foremost fire scene investigator in the British Empire," Dorothy replied.

"But he's not the foremost chemist. We have to go back to Mott and beg him to give us a real chemist."

"Damn it, Pell," Mott responded when Pell made his latest demand. "Do you fully comprehend how many hoops I had to jump through to get you Rethoret?"

"Yes, Colonel."

"No, I don't think you do. I leaned on a dozen contacts to learn the man existed. I had to disturb the Home Secretary on Boxing Day morning, burst into 10 Downing Street unannounced so the PM's personal secretary might cable the PM's Principal Private Secretary, in Washington with the PM, to beg Churchill to call the Prime Minister of Canada. All the while, the PM was preparing to address the U.S. Congress. Then I had to convince the Canadians to quietly put Rethoret on an immediate transatlantic flight so the word didn't get out."

"I very much appreciate everything you did."

"Then show your appreciation by shutting up about chemistry professors," said Mott.

"I would, Colonel, if Rethoret knew what we needed to know about chemistry, but he doesn't."

Mott gauged Pell's resolve. Mildred Tate's death had changed him. It was more personal now, and Mott could see it. "I'll see what I can do," he said at last. "But under no circumstances may you take matters into your own hands."

Mott ushered Pell from his office before further words could be spoken. Dorothy was waiting just outside the door.

"Miss Tanner," Mott said. "Please take our friend out dancing tonight. He needs a diversion."

"Yes, sir."

"You weren't listening at keyholes, Miss Tanner?"

"No, Colonel."

After Mott closed his door, Dorothy turned to Pell. "So? What did he say?"

"You didn't hear?"

"I wasn't listening."

"What kind of lousy spook are you?"

They walked on together. "You know why he thinks you need a diversion, don't you?" said Dorothy.

"Because of Mildred."

"Because you've become too personally involved."

"I'm not saying anything new."

"You're no good to him if it gets personal."

"Personal gives you focus," said Pell.

"Personal clouds your thinking," Dorothy replied. "We need to catch these people."

"And I don't want that?"

"No. Since Mildred died, you want to kill them."

Lew Stone and his band were playing at The Dorchester. Pell wasn't much of a dancer, but he did enjoy good music, and Stone's swing style interested him. It was a more genteel version of swing, lacking the drive of the best American swing bands, but magnetic in its own way. The music's gentility also encouraged marginal dancers to throw caution to the wind.

Dancing also afforded Pell an opportunity to speak privately with Dorothy. Couples at adjoining tables had prying ears, as did taxi drivers and strangers on the street. The combination of close contact and constant, spinning movement on the dance floor impeded eavesdropping.

"I got a letter from Alfred French," Pell said.

"I noticed the Edinburgh postmark," she replied.

"He's in London. Arrived today. Staying at the University Club though New Year's. Invited me to call him. To go to dinner."

"You can't," Dorothy said.

"Why not?"

"Mott told you not to take matters into your own hands."

"And you said you weren't listening," Pell chided.

"We spooks rarely answer the 'were you listening?' question with an honest answer."

"Having dinner is not taking anything into my own hands except a fork."

"You can't talk to French."

"Mott lets me speak to French as long as I don't speak out of turn. I have no intention of speaking out of turn."

"Then why go at all?" Dorothy asked.

"To keep our relationship on friendly terms. To keep the channels of communication open. Who knows what Mott will finally decide?" said Pell.

"You're playing with fire."

"There's no harm in playing with fire when ashes are the only thing you own."

Dorothy and Pell stepped outside The Dorchester and began walking up Park Lane toward Marble Arch at the northeast corner of Hyde Park. It was a cold and windy night, with the temperature dipping below the freezing mark. Just as dancing provides an acceptable reason to hold another close, so does walking in the cold. Pell could wrap Dorothy in his arms, not romantically, but in the name of chivalry. And to resist an act of chivalry would be downright impolite.

The two clearly were growing closer by the day. Pell's conscious fidelity to his absent wife remained strong, but everything around him whispered reminders of life's fragility. War doesn't breed intimacy merely because inhibition becomes pointless; it breeds intimacy because people fear dying alone.

It would have been so easy for either to suggest that, with the freezing temperature and swirling winds, the ordeal of a journey home was too formidable to attempt. They already were in the shadow of a luxury hotel. One room couldn't be that expensive. Under the circumstances, the other probably would have agreed.

However, neither spoke. Instead, they kept walking, intertwined but silent.

18. Dinner at the University Club

What the University Club spent on food it saved on electricity. The foyer was dimly lit, as were the hallways, lounges, and dining room. With dark mahogany walls and ceilings as a background, reading a Club menu required the assistance of a cigarette lighter. Unfortunately, Pell didn't smoke. So he left the ordering to Alfred, confident that dishes like "mock duck" — or "mock" anything else — were unlikely University Club dinner fare.

"What brings you to London?" Pell asked.

"A few errands," French replied.

"You're not staying at home?" French's home was on Gower Street in Bloomsbury.

"It's sublet for the term," said French. "Besides, senior faculty can stay here for less than it costs me to heat up a cold house in winter, even for a few days."

"Elsa must have stayed in Edinburgh then?" The University Club was a famous male-only province.

"Yes. I shan't tell her about tonight's meal. She'd be green with envy."

The waiter served asparagus soup, followed by pâté de foie gras.

"I had an additional reason for coming," French said. "I thought you might be of help to me, Anthony."

"In what way?"

French lowered his voice. In the semi-darkness, his

words assumed an ethereal quality. "Do you know anyone at Scotland Yard? I assume you consult with someone about police procedure for your books, in the same way you speak with me."

"Yes," Pell whispered back.

"I have information I feel it's my duty to report, but don't know to whom. I thought you might guide me, or arrange a meeting."

"Information about what?" Pell didn't want to bother his Scotland Yard contacts, or go to Stuart MacDonald, over nonsense.

"A German graduate student of mine. I think he may be involved in something subversive. Bruno — that's his name, Bruno Danziger. He's a brilliant chemist, but he never participates in university life, has no British friends as far as I know, and travels to London most weekends for reasons he refuses to disclose."

"That doesn't make him a subversive," Pell replied.

"And he's been experimenting with chlorine dioxide."

Pell looked puzzled. "What the hell is chlorine dioxide?" he asked.

"A harmless disinfectant when mixed with water, especially water in a swimming pool. But when applied to a porous surface and allowed to dry, it becomes highly volatile."

"Meaning?"

"Meaning it bursts into flames."

"And, let me guess, you checked with the athletic department and your grad student doesn't treat any of the University's swimming pools." French had piqued Pell's interest about Bruno Danziger.

"He doesn't work for the athletic department," said French. "He paints the chlorine dioxide on various surfaces, allows them to dry overnight in an opaque metal cabinet, and in the morning sets the surfaces on fire."

"He *sets* things on fire? I thought you said this chemical simply bursts into flames."

"He sets the samples on fire by opening the metal cabinet door," said French. "Exposure to light sets the treated substance on fire."

If an opaque cabinet worked, thought Pell, why not an opaque parcel box? "Is it dangerous, or more like your flash paper?"

"Nitrocellulose? No, not at all like nitrocellulose. Chlorine dioxide can be extremely dangerous. It depends on the type of surface, the area of surface, and the proximity to other material that will nurture the flame."

"Like the magnesium in an incendiary bomb," Pell offered.

"Exactly."

When Dorothy and Pell arrived at work the next day, Pell's suit pocket held a small photograph of Bruno Danziger and a copy of Danziger's University of London registration form bearing his East London address and other descriptive information. Alfred French had given him both on the promise that Pell would brief his friends at Scotland Yard. Pell went to Mott's office first, knowing that he first had to explain his dinner meeting the night before.

"It was just dinner, Colonel," Pell said. "I had no intention of discussing anything about our case, about chemistry, about anything scientific. It was to be purely social, an opportunity to keep on good terms with Alfred in the unlikely event you changed your mind about him."

"Highly unlikely event," Mott replied.

"He brought this up all on his own. He assumed I knew policemen — "

"Why would he assume that?"

"Because I write books about a Scotland Yard inspector. He knows I go to a chemistry professor when my books need answers about chemistry. He assumed, correctly I might add, that I consult with the police when I need information about police work."

Mott took the photograph and registration form from Pell. "Tell me precisely what he told you about the German."

Pell recounted the entire hushed, unlit conversation. "According to your professor friend, the German comes to London only on weekends?" Mott asked after Pell finished.

"He said Danziger comes to London most weekends."

"But our fires are during the week. They happen only rarely on weekends."

"I'm not suggesting that Danziger actually delivers the

incendiaries. But he could make them, or at least design them, for whomever does."

Mott stared at the face of Bruno Danziger, glancing periodically at the biographical information on the University of London form. Was this the picture of a saboteur?

"Take these to Giles and Stuart MacDonald," he said finally. "Tell them I want a tail put on the German. I don't care if it's an MI5 tail or a Special Branch tail, as long as he's followed from the minute he steps off the Edinburgh train at King's Cross until he steps back on."

Pell rose to leave, then looked back at Mott. "I did good, right?" he asked.

"Let's put it this way," Mott replied. "So far you've given me insufficient cause to charge you with treason."

19. An Inspirational Eulogy

Several dozen mourners entered St. Michael's Church in Camden Town for Mildred Tate's funeral. It wasn't a large gathering, but it was much larger than Pell once feared. Despite the wires he'd sent, Pell knew he might be sitting alone. When Dorothy and her father announced that both were coming ("Lately, I've been to more funerals than picture shows," William Tanner said sadly), Pell was relieved. Three mourners at least outnumbered the two required attendees: Father Hogarth and Mildred.

Pell prepared something to say, even to empty pews. He hadn't known Mildred long, but she deserved a few kind words from someone who was fond of her. He talked about how they met, how lovely Mildred was to work with, and the care with which she meticulously organized the life of someone she hardly knew. He ended with a wish they could have been together longer—followed by a perfunctory request, added extemporaneously once he saw how many others were in the church, that if anyone had anything else to say, to please step forward.

A man somewhere in his late sixties, wearing a suit that no longer fit him properly (kept, no doubt, either for these occasions or for delivery to the undertaker), rose from his pew, stepped over two others to reach the aisle, and approached the pulpit.

"My name is Lionel Braithwaite," he said to the assemblage. "Mildred Tate and I worked together at Simpkin Marshall for eighteen years. She was a wonderful woman. Books were her passion. Books were her family. And she got to live most of her life surrounded by books. Thousands of them in that warehouse in Paternoster Row.

"They let the employees borrow whatever books they wanted as long as they kept them clean. Mildred always had a book in her handbag. How she cried when the Germans bombed Simpkin Marshall almost exactly a year ago. All those books destroyed. 'What did these books ever do to them,' she said. It's so fitting that she found employment with a famous author after Simpkin Marshall closed.

"I'll always remember Mildred scurrying to pick up the latest book she could find, and then sitting at the tea break with her nose in that book. It's a very fond memory."

As Lionel Braithwaite stepped down from the pulpit to return to his pew, the picture he painted of Mildred echoed in Pell's mind's eye. Suddenly, he knew.

"Let's go," he said, leaning over to Dorothy.

"We can't go yet. The service isn't over. And what about the burial?"

"No time for that," Pell said as he gathered his coat and scarf. "I know."

"Know what?"

"I know how Mildred died. I know how they all died."

"How?"

"You and William meet me outside. Hail a taxi. I have

to find a phone. We'll take William home and then you and I are off to St. James's Street."

Before Dorothy could say another word, Pell was down the aisle and out the front door of St. Michael's. He found a phone box on Camden Road and dialed Giles Curtis.

"Giles? Pell. You've got to get word to Stuart. Tell him that Danziger may be headed to Paternoster Row. If he is, it's to meet whomever he's working with. He couldn't have done all this on his own. This may be our chance."

"How do you know?" Curtis asked.

"Because all the pieces fit. Look, Dorothy and I are headed in. I'll explain it all when I get there. Just tell Stuart: Paternoster Row."

"Any particular address?"

"I don't know, but my guess is the old Simpkin Marshall warehouse."

Dorothy was waiting by a taxi in front of the church.

"Dad said to go on without him, that he's perfectly capable of finding his way home on his own."

The two jumped in the back seat of the taxi and Pell gave the driver the St. James's Street address.

"Now what's this all about?" Dorothy asked.

"It's about what an idiot I've been." Pell could not believe his own stupidity. The answer had been bouncing around his head all along. For longer than he'd been on the "Silent Blitz" team. From before he first met Raymond Mott. He'd taken long walks around Maida Vale with the answer.

He'd known the answer before he'd even heard the question. He'd known the answer since that October night at the Detection Club, when he'd asked Agatha whether there was anyone she'd wanted to make her least likely suspect, but couldn't figure out how to do it.

He'd known the answer ever since Agatha motioned for him to lean over, placed her mouth near his ear, and whispered the two words: "the reader."

Shortly after 5:00 p.m., Bruno Danziger stepped off the train from Edinburgh at King's Cross under the watchful eye of Stuart MacDonald and two fellow Special Branch detectives. He boarded a District Line underground train headed east, finally exiting at Stepney Green. He walked up Alderney Road, turned left at Bancroft Road near Mile End Hospital and Queen Mary College, and entered a building on Bancroft corresponding to the address on his University registration form. Another Special Branch detective was positioned on the first-floor landing with a clear view of the door to Danziger's flat.

"Go up the apples and have a butcher's," the detective was instructed. To anyone born within the sound of the bells of St. Mary-le-Bow Church on Cheapside this meant: "Go up the stairs and have a look."

Danziger unlocked his flat door, reached down, picked up an envelope lying on the floor just inside, and closed the door behind him.

***

"It's a book," Pell told the team at MI5 headquarters, with only MacDonald absent. "He's putting a book through the mail slot—a book that ignites when someone inside opens it to read it."

"How does it ignite?" Rethoret asked.

"With chlorine dioxide and magnesium. The pages are treated with chlorine dioxide. The covers are lined with thin sheets of magnesium. When the book is opened, the chlorine dioxide is exposed to light. Chlorine dioxide bursts into flame when it's exposed to light. This ignites not only the book but the magnesium sheeting. Magnesium intensifies the heat and fire, just like with an incendiary bomb."

Giles Curtis turned to Harry Rethoret. "Is what he's saying possible?" he asked.

"I don't know. It's not an accelerant I'm familiar with."

"You said it yourself, Harry," Pell said. "It has to be something that ignites inches from someone's face. I realized it at Mildred's funeral, when a friend described her as someone who always had her nose in a book. And I remembered her body in the morgue. Face gone, hands gone. That's where the blast happened. That's why the victims were in chairs or on beds. They were about to read a book."

For the first time, Giles Curtis did not minimize or quibble with Pell's theory.

"Another thing Mildred's friend mentioned was how eagerly she rushed around trying to find a new book to read. And it occurred to me how rare a new book is in Britain these days. People are reading recipes, they're so hungry for reading material. A free new book comes through the mail slot? Who won't open it?"

"And that's why you sent Stuart to Paternoster Row? The publishing houses? Where someone can bind hundreds of books to use as incendiaries?" Giles asked.

"I doubt that's what they're doing. I'm sure they're using existing books. We lost dozens of book warehouses in Paternoster Row last December. Millions of books were destroyed. But not all of them. I'll bet, if you combed through what's left of those warehouses, you'd find hundreds of books, a little the worse for wear perhaps, but good enough to get someone to open the cover. Some obscure title no one was likely to have read before. Simpkin Marshall had thousands of unsold books."

"If this chemical ignites when it's exposed to light, why doesn't the book ignite in the warehouse?" Rethoret asked.

"My guess is that the treatments were applied at night in the dark," said Pell. "And then the book was wrapped in something opaque, so it couldn't ignite until it was opened."

"The saboteur worked in total darkness?" Giles asked.

"Trained properly, it's certainly possible," Pell replied.

"Blind people do it routinely," Dorothy added.

20. 32 Paternoster Row

Paternoster Row was pitch black as Bruno Danziger, armed with a bright flashlight—a torch—climbed over the still uncollected rubble from a year ago in search of the building number he had committed to memory. He found the correct door and went inside.

Bruno was met with a shouted: "Schaltet sie das licht aus!" ("Turn off the light!"). This was followed closely by a second man saying, "Willst du uns alle umbringen?" ("Do you want to kill us all?"). Two German voices demanding secrecy and fearing discovery. Bruno knew he was in the right place. He didn't have long to enjoy his discovery.

Seconds later, Bruno Danziger was in the clutches of powerful arms, bound in handcuffs, and before he understood what was happening, thrown into the back of a truck. Two more men, similarly bound, were thrown in beside him. One was tall and lean, the other short with a badly scarred face. The tall one was whispering short descriptive phrases in German, as if the short one could not see for himself.

The next morning, the entire "Silent Blitz" team, accompanied by Raymond Mott, returned to the abandoned Simpkin Marshall warehouse at 32 Paternoster Row, site of the previous night's arrests. They found a small work area with some bedding nearby. The work table had rolls of magnesium sheeting and a canister of a chemical liquid that, when tested, would likely prove to be chlorine dioxide. Fresh burn spots on the table signified that some excess chlorine dioxide had ignited with the morning light.

There were also assorted brushes, metal shears, scissors, rolls of heavy brown paper wrapping, and a pot of glue. And next to the work table stood two high stacks of fairly thin books. The books in one stack were all wrapped in heavy brown paper. The books in the other apparently were awaiting treatment.

"And now we know why most people did not open their books until nighttime, until they sat or lay down ready to read," Pell said. Encircling each of the wrapped books, like a seal, was a red and white paper strip bearing the words: "DO NOT BREAK THIS SEAL UNLESS YOU PLEDGE TO MAINTAIN THE SECRETS OF THE BOOK INSIDE." The seal was just enough to deter the recipient from unwrapping the book before committing to read it.

"Go through this once more for me, Mr. Pell," Mott asked.

"Certainly, Colonel. The saboteurs treat the book as we discussed, wrap it, put this seal around it, and trail the local postman, slipping one in the mail slot of every fourth or fifth house in a given area.

"The homeowner returns, sees what apparently is a long-awaited new book, reads the warning, puts it aside until later in the evening or bedtime, takes a seat, and then breaks the seal and opens the book.

"As soon as the book is opened, light hits the chemically treated pages, causing a bright and powerful flash. Flames burst up. Face, hair, skin, and clothing catch fire as the magnesium begins to glow white hot. The victim is overcome. The book drops to the floor. The fire spreads to objects nearby: bedding, carpets, furniture. Within moments, the entire room is on fire. And the fire grows from there. Is that about right, Harry?"

"I imagine so," said Rethoret.

"And any book would do?" Mott asked.

"Any thin book. Fully outfitted with magnesium sheeting and wrapped in thick brown paper, it still must be thin enough to fit through a mail slot. The more obscure and unfamiliar the title, the more likely the homeowner was to start reading the book that very night."

Dorothy went over to the pile of fresh, untreated books, grabbed one of the thin volumes off the top, and handed it to Pell.

"And the winner," he said, "is *Last Train to Gidleigh.*"

21. Pell Returns to the Detection Club

Pell looked forward to this evening's Detection Club meeting. His investigation was over; his life could begin to return to normal. He still needed to find a place to live, but was in no great hurry to leave the Tanners. Pell did have to buy a second-hand tuxedo for tonight's dinner, but at least had someone to help him with his bowtie.

Dinners were for members only, or else he would have invited Dorothy to accompanying him. Yes, it would have caused some comment. His professional friends all knew Claire. But his conscience was clear. Then again, how would he have introduced her? "The woman who took me in" would have been misunderstood. "My friend at MI5" would stifle interesting conversation. Maybe it was fortunate Detection Club rules were as they were.

Pell's principal excitement this evening, however, did not involve Dorothy. Tonight gave Pell the chance to tell Agatha that he had solved her little problem. After all, who ignited each of the deadly "Silent Blitz" fires? The *readers* of *Last Train to Gidleigh.*

Beyond telling Agatha, he knew the solution would make a sensational mystery novel. The quintessential great idea. A book whose title had nothing to do with the story, where a lethal flash fire occurs as soon as the reader opens the cover. Not actually, but in descriptive language. Not a literal fire, but a literary fire. On the first inside page, before even the title page.

It would be a book in which the book itself proved to be an important character. The core of the story would be set into motion merely by the reader beginning to read. And best of all, the reader would read the solution before beginning the mystery — and never know it.

But, of course, he'd never write such a book. He wouldn't because he couldn't. He couldn't even tell Agatha how he'd arrived at the answer to her problem.

He could do none of these things because he'd signed the Official Secrets Act.

22. HAM, CAMP 020

In peacetime, Latchmere House was a sprawling Victorian mansion along the Thames in the center of Ham Common, a suburb southwest of London. In wartime, Latchmere House was the home of Camp 020, the MI5 interrogation center.

It was to Camp 020 that the truck brought Bruno Danziger, Rolf Bahn, and Friedrich Kapellmann following their arrests in Paternoster Row. And it was at Camp 020 where their ultimate fates would be determined. One of two verdicts was possible: they would be asked to betray the Fatherland and spy for Britain, or be executed. As Giles Curtis had said, "We either turn them or hang them."

The three were fortunate that their arrests had occurred in silence and darkness. MI5 had no use for a German spy known to have been arrested, because the Germans would never trust a spy who had been arrested and mysteriously released. Spies spotted parachuting into a farmer's field and arrested by rural police on the report of a local citizen, for example, stood no chance of escaping the rope or the firing squad. A German agent's secret apprehension was his only potential salvation.

The responsibility for determining through which door Danziger, Bahn, and Kapellmann would pass fell upon Giles Curtis, Stuart MacDonald, and Dorothy Tanner. Rolf Bahn a/k/a The Postman was the easiest call. Bahn had no special skills; his sole job was to slide a wrapped book through a letter box and not get caught doing it. He had no important contacts. He'd never met his German handler in Britain face to face or spoken to him on the phone. Their communications had been through a series of mail and parcel drops. That's how Bahn and Kapellmann collected the chemical supplies they needed, were instructed on how to build the incendiary devices, and knew where a cache of ready-to-use books and other materials were located. All messages had been destroyed upon receipt, as instructed.

The last message Bahn collected from the ever-changing mail drop told him to expect a nighttime visit at Paternoster Row to arrange his and Kapellmann's escape from England. They'd completed their mission; the risks attending further fires exceeded the benefits. He assumed Danziger was this contact, but only because he appeared at their squat when expected and understood German.

In addition, as Bahn was not an agent reporting intelligence back to Germany, he was not someone who could serve the British cause by reporting misinformation, fed by MI5, to the Abwehr.

No, Bahn was useless to His Majesty's Government. He was destined for the gallows at either Wandsworth or Pentonville.

Friedrich Kapellmann a/k/a The Bat was a closer call. He was a demolition expert, although a mishap with an experimental grenade in 1939 disfigured his face, blinded him, and limited his value to the Third Reich. He had not designed the incendiary devices Bahn delivered; he did not know anything about chlorine dioxide before Bahn read him the manufacturing instructions he was told to follow and then destroy. Fittingly, he did so by coating the message in chlorine dioxide, letting it dry, and sensing it ignite at daybreak: the hiss of the initial burst, the heat of the flames, the smell of burnt paper, the feel of the cool ashes.

Like Bahn, Kapellmann knew nothing of Danziger.

Was Kapellmann's knowledge of German munitions worth keeping him alive? Could he be fully debriefed by the Army and then hanged? This was not a decision MI5 or Special Branch could make on their own.

Bruno Danziger was an entirely different matter. Bahn and Kapellmann confessed to everything; Danziger confessed to nothing. He said he went to 32 Pasternoster Row that night because a note he'd found inside his front door told him to do so. He didn't have the note; he was also told to destroy it. He was vague about why he went and what he expected to find. But the Special Branch detective surveilling his flat door corroborated that Danziger did pick up a piece of paper just after he entered. The detective could not see its content; as far as he knew, it could have been a rent bill.

"Let me speak to him," Dorothy Tanner asked.

"Planning to do the Dance of the Seven Veils?" Curtis inquired. "Think that will loosen his tongue?"

"No, Giles. But so far the high-handed approach hasn't

gotten us very far. Perhaps a softer voice will."

"I have no objection," said Stuart MacDonald. "What's the worst that can happen?"

"She can give away the store," said Curtis.

"If I did promise anything—that he wouldn't hang, for example—would you feel bound to honor my promise?" asked Dorothy.

"Absolutely not," Curtis said.

"Then what are you worried about?"

Curtis had no answer. "There's one condition," he said finally. "That you tell him Bahn and Kapellmann confessed and named him as the person running their operation."

"They said precisely the opposite," said Dorothy.

"Take it or leave it."

"Good morning, Bruno," Dorothy said entering the interrogation room.

"Good morning," Danziger responded in a soft German accent. He didn't look at Dorothy, preferring to stare at a spot on the wall.

"I don't think this will take very long. Your two friends have told us everything. We know you were in charge of your little ring of saboteurs."

"That's a lie!"

"Not according to them."

Danziger turned to his inquisitor. "They're lying to try to save their own necks."

"Come on, Bruno. You were with them in their work-shop at night, in the dark."

"That's where I was told — "

"Yes, yes, we've heard it before," said Dorothy. "The note on the floor of your flat."

"It's the truth."

"Do you always go wherever anonymous notes direct you to go? Anonymous notes you immediately destroy?"

"I'd been expecting this note. But not for the reasons you think." His eyes examined the floor, as if he had lost some change.

"Were you expecting to find a couple of Germans when you got there?"

"Not for the reasons you think."

"So you *were* expecting to find German agents?"

"German refugees, not German agents," Danziger said.

"Is that what they're called in the Abwehr handbook?" Dorothy shot back.

"You wouldn't understand."

"Try me."

Danziger faced Dorothy again. "I was looking for in-formation about my family in Germany. I was told to expect to hear from some refugees who might know what became of them." Danziger took a handkerchief from his shirt pocket and wiped his face.

"Refugees you had to meet in the dark, in a bombed-out building?"

"Refugees who may not have had the proper paperwork to be in this country."

"You're a chemist, aren't you, Bruno?" Dorothy asked.

"I'm a chemistry student at the University of London."

"Are you familiar with chlorine dioxide?"

"Somewhat."

"Tell me about it."

"It's a cleanser," Danziger said. "A disinfectant."

"Always?" asked Dorothy.

"In its liquid form, yes. When its moisture evaporates, it becomes unstable."

"It ignites?"

"It can."

"If exposed to light, for example?"

"I've read that's true," said Danziger, "but I've never seen it happen."

"Haven't you experimented with chlorine dioxide?"

"What do you mean 'experimented'?"

"What do you think I mean?" Dorothy replied.

"You could mean experiments specifically about chlorine dioxide. Or you could mean using chlorine dioxide in an experiment about something else."

"Why don't you give me both answers?"

"I have never experimented about chlorine dioxide itself. If I ever used chlorine dioxide in some other experiment, I don't remember."

"Why aren't you in the Army, Bruno?"

"You have to be here five years to be eligible for citizenship. I've only been here four years."

"You could have volunteered. Don't you love your adopted country?"

"I do. Very much. More, apparently, than it loves me." He paused. "I wanted to complete my degree. I thought I would be more useful as a scientist than as a soldier."

"Why weren't you interned as an enemy alien?"

"I was summoned to a tribunal. They reviewed my case and determined that I was not a security risk."

"Class C?" she asked.

"Class C."

"Do you know why?"

"Yes."

"Because you're such a brilliant chemistry student?"

"No."

"Then why?"

"Because I am a Jew," Danziger said.

Danziger's interrogation room was bugged. Giles and Stuart monitored Dorothy's interview. When Danziger said what he said, Giles turned to Stuart and asked, "Why in God's name didn't he tell us this before?"

"Because he doesn't trust us. He doesn't know." Mac-Donald reached for the ashtray to stub out his unfiltered Woodbine "gasper."

"Know what?"

"Whether we hate Jews, too."

Meanwhile, Dorothy felt a rush of excitement. She'd succeeded where others had not. She continued her interview for just a few more minutes, clarifying that Danziger made his weekend trips from Edinburgh to London to spend Shabbat — the Jewish Sabbath — among a small circle of London Jews he had met shortly after his arrival in Britain. Other than these few friends, he stayed alone much of the time. Jews were not often welcomed, he said, and his experience in Germany had made him suspicious of — well, pretty much everyone.

He believed some, maybe all, of his remaining family in Germany were arrested by the Nazis, but wasn't sure. Friends of friends had promised him further word if they could locate anyone who knew more. That's what he thought the note under his door was all about. His friends knew he returned home weekly; slipping a note under his door was easier than trying to reach him in Edinburgh.

Curtis, MacDonald, and Tanner left immediately for St. James's Street to report this new information to Colonel Mott. Of course, Danziger's claim would have to be confirmed before Mott could report this development to Petrie, Morrison, and perhaps even Churchill. But the team at Camp 020 knew deception when they heard it. They had little doubt that Danziger was telling the truth.

23. FRENCH CONNECTION

"Boy, did Alfred get his wires crossed," Pell said when Dorothy told him Bruno Danziger's revelation. Pell still was a member of the team and subject to the Official Secrets Act; nonetheless, Dorothy kept her recap to the essentials.

"Are you sure about that?" she asked.

"What does that mean?"

"Mott thinks it's awfully strange that we only learned of Bruno Danziger, and then tailed and arrested him, because of the tip your friend gave us."

"No, you arrested Danziger because he went to Paternoster Row in the dark of night, to rendezvous with two confessed saboteurs."

"And who sent him there?" Dorothy responded.

"Assuming someone did send him there," said Pell.

"According to French, Danziger was using chlorine dioxide to set things on fire. If you believe Bruno, and I do, that never happened. He's never even seen a chlorine dioxide fire. To quote Stuart MacDonald, 'I'm smelling an oven full of pork pies.'"

Pell wrinkled his brow quizzically. "Spend more time in the East End, Anthony," Dorothy added. "'Pork pies' means 'lies.'"

Pell was unmoved. "The only reason you're crediting Danziger over Alfred is that you believe Danziger is a Jew."

"He is a Jew," said Dorothy. "It's in official records. His

friends confirm it. His rabbi confirms it. The items in his flat confirm it. There's no doubt he's Jewish."

"Okay, but that doesn't make the rest of his story true. Who says a Jew can't work for the Abwehr?"

"He can't."

"Not voluntarily, maybe. But someone whose family is being held hostage?" Pell suggested. "People will do a lot of uncharacteristic things to save their family. And Danziger says his family is being held in Germany."

"It's not possible," she said.

"And what better alibi if you get arrested?" Pell added.

"No," she repeated. "No Nazi trusts a Jew enough to use him as a spy."

"Why would Alfred tell us about Danziger if he didn't think what he was saying was true?" Pell asked Dorothy the next morning over breakfast. "Why would he voluntarily inject himself into our case if he had something to hide? He'd keep his head down and stay as far away from us as possible."

Dorothy poured the coffee while Pell made the toast. "Maybe he wanted a tidy way to shut down a successful operation that left no loose ends wandering free around England," she said. "Maybe Bahn and Kapellmann were of no further use to the Abwehr and he wanted MI5 to dispose of them so he didn't have to. He couldn't tip us off to the two saboteurs, so he created someone we would follow, and led him to the viper's nest."

"That's pretty far-fetched, don't you think?" Pell said.

"Watch it, Anthony. You're starting to sound like Giles Curtis. I've said nothing that you wouldn't have said in my place, if we weren't talking about someone you considered a friend."

"But that's just the point," Pell said, reaching for the sugar bowl. "He *is* a friend. Someone I've known a long time. Someone I've trusted for a long time. That carries weight. It does with me, at least."

Dorothy stopped spreading her toast with mock orange marmalade, a neighbor's Christmas gift made from apples and carrots. She turned in her chair to look Pell squarely in the eye. "But it can't—not if you want to stay in the room," she said.

"What does *that* mean?"

"It means that Mott wants you back. You *do* know French, and that knowledge is valuable. But Mott expects you to put your biases aside."

Fewer people gathered in the room at 57-58 St. James's Street to discuss the current state of their investigation than participated before the arrests on Paternoster Row. The services of Keith Hall, Leonard Tomlinson, and Bennett Weston no longer were required and they'd returned to their National Fire Service duties. Likewise, Harry Rethoret was flown back to Montreal as quietly as he had been summoned to London.

That left Giles Curtis, Stuart MacDonald, Dorothy Tanner, Anthony Pell, plus one addition — Colonel Raymond Mott, who thought it high time he took a seat at the conference table.

"My assessment is this," Mott began. "Either Bruno Danziger is lying or Alfred French is lying. Both cannot be telling the truth." Mott turned to Pell. "French gave you a detailed account of Danziger's use of that chemical — what is it?"

"Chlorine dioxide," Pell said.

"Right. While Danziger maintains he never did any of these experiments, that he's never even seen this chemical ignite in sunlight. French also painted a picture of Danziger as a mysterious loner who took suspicious, unexplained trips to London. Meanwhile, Danziger tells us — why don't you repeat what you told me, Miss Tanner?"

"Yes, sir. Bruno told me that Professor French knew he was worried about his family's condition in Germany. He talked to French about it. He asked if French knew any German scientists who might have helpful contacts."

"Yet French told you none of this," Mott said to Pell, who clearly was being singled out for Mott's attention. Pell was beginning to feel like the lone holdout in a jury room.

"According to Bruno," Dorothy added, "French told him he knew no German scientists."

"Or none he still communicates with," Pell threw in. "That could be what he meant."

"And French's last trip to London coincided with when someone slipped the rendezvous note under Danziger's door," said Mott.

"What's the purpose of this, Colonel?" Pell asked. "You've obviously made your mind up."

"Not true, Mr. Pell. I find these circumstances extremely suspicious, but I do not consider them proof. And I want proof. So my question is: how do we prove that Alfred French either did, or did not, instigate these fires? Any suggestions, Mr. Pell? If you want to exonerate your friend, now is the time."

Pell knew Mott was right. The truth was the truth. Pell's defense of Alfred French was conditioned on his innocence. If not, then French had helped set Mildred on fire. He thought for a moment before speaking.

"Hamlet wanted proof Claudius murdered his father. So he invited Claudius to a play, *The Murder of Gonzago.* In the play is a murder identical to the one Hamlet believed Claudius committed. Hamlet's plan was to watch Claudius' reaction. 'If he but blench, I know my course,' Hamlet says."

"You're suggesting we invite Professor French to a play?" Giles laced his question with a few drops of sarcasm.

"Not exactly," said Pell.

"Thank God," said Curtis.

"I'm proposing we show Alfred something to gauge his reaction. I'm proposing we give him a wrapped and banded copy of *Last Train to Gidleigh.*"

The conference room went silent. No one was sure who was supposed to speak next. Stuart MacDonald finally took the initiative.

"If French is the one, he's sure to recognize the red and white band," he said. "Those were printed before they went to Bahn and Kapellmann, so both say."

"We wouldn't give him an incendiary copy, would we?" Dorothy asked. "That'll set him on fire only if he's *not* the one."

"We'd use a dummy copy, identically wrapped, but with the magnesium sheeting so the weight is right," said Pell.

"How do we explain our having the book?" Giles asked.

"It came through my mail slot, my letter box" Pell suggested. "My secretary put it in a pile. I didn't see it for a while, and decided to bring it with me to Edinburgh in case I wanted something to read. 'Of course, Alfred, you're more than welcome to it.'"

"Doesn't he know about your house and your secretary?" asked Mott.

"No. I didn't want to discuss with him anything about the London fires."

Mott paused. "It would have to be in a public setting, so several of us can watch him react."

Mott disliked giving formal approval to anything. This would have to do.

24. BACK TO THE CAFÉ ROYAL

Within 48 hours, Pell was back aboard the Flying Scotsman. This time he wasn't alone. Dorothy, Stuart, and Giles were with him. It would be their job to observe Alfred French from various vantage points — to see "if he but blench," as Hamlet put it, when Pell invited him to open *Last Train to Gidleigh*.

Pell and Dorothy sat in adjoining seats on the journey north. Between the two was Pell's leather briefcase containing notes he intended to share with French about the Royal Bank of Scotland. Protruding from the case's rear section was a parcel wrapped in heavy brown paper and encircled by a red and white warning strip.

"You do have to begin thinking about finding a home," said Dorothy.

"Are you kicking me out?"

"No. But you have a family. They may wish to visit. You need a proper home."

"But you have a neighbor who supplies you with mock orange marmalade," Pell said.

"I'll get you a jar."

Pell turned to look out the carriage window as the train passed Durham Cathedral. "An empty house is lonely," he said.

"So is a house where two people constantly keep their distance from one another," replied Dorothy.

He turned back to Dorothy. "I'm sorry."

"So am I."

Pell had taken a table in the center of the Café Royal and sat facing the front door. His leather briefcase was at his feet. MacDonald was at the bar, Curtis in a booth, and Dorothy in the cloakroom doorway. Each had an unobstructed view of the chair opposite Pell's.

As always, French arrived exactly at the appointed hour, spotted Pell, and moved toward his table.

"Do observatories set clocks based on your comings and goings?" Pell asked, mocking French's punctuality.

"An appointment is a promise, and I keep my promises," said French with a smile, setting down his umbrella.

Pell ordered two pints of beer and the men settled down to chat. "Thank you so much for seeing me again," Pell began.

"It's my pleasure. Were you able to speak to your friend at Scotland Yard?"

"Yes, I spoke to him and gave him the information about your student."

"Excellent."

"I don't know what will come of it," Pell said.

"I understand, but at least I've done my civic duty."

"I wanted to speak to you again about my story. I have an appointment tomorrow morning at the Royal Bank of Scotland. They've permitted me to see their vault in action."

"Isn't that unusual?" French asked.

"The advantage of having a well-known association with locked rooms." As he said this, Pell smoothly lifted his briefcase onto the café table with the front leather flap facing in his direction for ease of opening. This meant that the rear section, with its protruding wrapped parcel and visible red and white sealing band, faced French. "I made a few notes I wanted to discuss with you," he said as he opened the leather flap, reached inside, and withdrew some papers.

French could not help but stare at the protruding parcel.

"When we met at the University Club," Pell continued, "you mentioned some chemical your student used that bursts into flames when exposed to light."

"Chlorine dioxide," French said, still eying the parcel.

"Right," said Pell. He closed the briefcase flap but the case refused to remain standing. Its interior was now empty and thus failed to counterbalance the full rear section. Accordingly, Pell removed the wrapped parcel and put it on the table between the two men. "My question is," Pell continued, "why not use chlorine dioxide on the contents of the safe deposit box?"

"Safe deposit box?" French sounded confused.

"In my story. The box with the papers that burst into flames?"

"Yes, yes. Of course."

"Why not use chlorine dioxide?"

"It's a possibility," said French. "It does require that you find an earlier opportunity to apply the chemical in liquid form, and leave enough time for the chemical to dry thoroughly inside the sealed box."

Pell began writing down French's instructions on a page of notes he'd removed from the briefcase. This pause in the conversation allowed French more time to contemplate the wrapped parcel with the red and white strip.

"Need a book to read?" Pell stopped writing to ask.

"Pardon?"

Pell indicated the parcel. "Someone shoved this through my letter box a week or so ago. It's been under a pile of mail ever since. I brought it with me in case I needed something to read, but with my visit to the bank tomorrow, I doubt I'll have any spare time. Consider it a thank-you present."

"It's very kind of you, but —"

"You know what my friends at the Detection Club say? They say that in Britain these days, it's easier to write a new book than to find a new book."

"How true," said French.

"Then again, it may not be your cup of tea. From the label I gather it's a novel with a secret twist. Feel free to take a look." Pell went back to his note-taking.

"That's very generous of you." French took the parcel from the table and stood it against the table leg near his feet.

"Anything else I should know about chlorine dioxide?" Pell asked.

"Not that I can think of at the moment." Making no attempt to be subtle, French slipped his fingers into his vest pocket, retrieved his pocket watch, and checked the time. "Oh, dear," he said, "I'm late for an appointment in my office."

"You? Late?" Pell said with feigned surprise.

"Unless I leave now, that is." French rose from his chair, shook Pell's hand, grabbed his umbrella, and left the café.

The wrapped parcel encircled by the red and white paper band remained resting against the table leg.

"He didn't take the book," MacDonald said. "Why would he thank you for the book, and then leave it behind? He wouldn't even open it when you invited him to."

"He kept staring at it all the time you were writing in your notebook," Dorothy added. "He recognized it."

"And making such a show of checking his watch?" said MacDonald. "He wanted out of here in the worst way."

"All true," said Pell. "But not proof of anything."

"I agree with Mr. Pell," said Curtis. "Suspicious, but not proof. Like Mott said."

"So what do we do now?" MacDonald asked.

"We could arrest him on suspicion and question him?" said Dorothy.

"Not without Mott's authority," said Curtis. "Mott barely authorized us to do this."

Pell was deep in thought. "I have an idea," he said at

last. He checked his wristwatch. "It's twenty past two. Can you three be in Alfred's office at three o'clock?" he said, writing an address on a slip of paper. "Not standing outside his office. At least one of you must be in the same room with Alfred at three o'clock precisely. I'm going to call him at three o'clock. Make sure he takes the call in your presence."

"What's going on?" MacDonald asked.

"You'll see," he said, packing his briefcase including the wrapped parcel. "If your suspicions are correct, his reaction will be impossible to miss."

25. Zero Hour

Pell and his companions left the Café Royal. Pell went in one direction, the others in another.

Within minutes, Pell reached his destination. He exchanged greetings, had a brief conversation, politely declined an invitation to share tea, made his excuses, and went on his way. Pell's burden was relieved somewhat by the brief visit.

Meanwhile, Giles, Stuart, and Dorothy found the address Pell gave them: the University building that housed Alfred French's office. On the way, they formulated a plan. It seemed unlikely that French would open his office to the three of them at once. Getting one person inside was the reasonable goal, and Dorothy was the most promising candidate. She was the youngest, and she was the easiest on the eye. French was less likely to resist the attentions of a pretty girl.

His office was on the second floor. It had a wooden door with a translucent glass window bearing Professor French's name and title. If MacDonald and Curtis stood on either side of the door, they might be able to hear what was going on inside.

It was 2:58 p.m. when Dorothy knocked.

"Come in," said the voice inside. So the door wasn't locked. This was a bonus. Dorothy could enter without French coming to the doorway and seeing into the hall.

She opened the door and walked in. "Professor?"

"Yes."

"I'm from the University office for faculty housing. Periodically, we check to make sure that our faculty is satisfied with its accommodations here in Edinburgh. We understand the inconvenience of your relocation but—"

The telephone rang.

French looked at the phone and then at Dorothy. "Will you excuse me?" he said.

"Certainly," she replied. But she never moved.

"Alfred? It's Anthony."

"Hello, Anthony."

"Won't be but a minute. I just called to tell you that you forgot the book I gave you in the café. Nothing to worry about. I took it over and gave it to Elsa."

Pell was right. French's reaction was unambiguous. He forgot entirely that Dorothy was in the room. He pushed down the plunger on the phone, cutting Pell off, and began to dial furiously.

"Elsa? Elsa? Did Anthony Pell give you a book wrapped in brown paper? Then whatever you do, don't remove that paper, do you hear me!"

That's as far as French got before MacDonald and Curtis came through his door.

26. ONE FINAL PLEA

Pell's final visit to Raymond Mott was ten days after he returned from Edinburgh.

By this time, Alfred French had spent over a week at Camp 020. Pell was shocked to learn from Dorothy that French had been working for the Germans since 1937. In the 1920's, he had joined a circle of European scientists and developed strong ties to its German members. He had come to believe in the superiority of the German mind, and that a German Europe was in the best interests of the cause of science.

"Germans revere science," French told Stuart MacDonald. "Germans revere scientists. What do the British revere? Inherited wealth, inherited titles, and dogs who chase and kill foxes. We are a frivolous country."

If French could ever be trusted — which was far from evident — he possessed enormous potential as a double agent, learning from his German counterparts their latest advances while feeding them misinformation about the Allies' weapons programs. If he could be trusted, his life likely would be spared. But that proviso could not be satisfied in the near term. In the near term, French would remain at Camp 020.

With French's arrest, Bruno Danziger was released. He would have to find another professor under whom to complete his graduate studies, but completed they would be. And in time, news of his family would arrive, although it was the news he least wanted to receive.

Pell's last visit to Mott was not merely to say good-bye. Pell had a request. A final plea.

"Colonel, I know I must obey the Official Secrets Act."

"Your grasp of the obvious is commendable, Mr. Pell."

"But what about after the war?" Pell asked.

"Your obligations under the Official Secrets Act do not expire. They never expire, I'm afraid."

"I would change the names of the principal characters, including yours. Including my own."

"I hardly see how that makes a difference."

"I think it does. Fiction isn't fact. I asked once before if I might write a novel based on my work here."

"And what was my answer?" Mott replied.

"You didn't answer. You asked, 'What do you think?'"

"You didn't find that response instructive?"

"I found it evasive," said Pell.

"That's unfortunate."

"But after the war —" Pell began.

"After the war," replied Mott, "you write whatever you think you're entitled to write. If you're then doing porridge in Wormwood Scrubs, you'll know you misjudged the situation."

Pell did leave the Tanners' home for one of his own. He found a place near Regent's Park. The war wouldn't last forever. The anti-aircraft guns dotting the park would be gone. The London Zoo would return, as would his girls. They'd enjoy walking to the zoo whenever they wanted.

Pell resumed his work for the BBC but, in his spare time, began a new Inspector Barnaby mystery. It was different from his prior books. This book began with a flash, a bright and powerful flash.

Whether it ever could be published, he did not know.

AFTERWORD

Last Train to Gidleigh is fiction. The "Silent Blitz" never happened. After the Blitz ended on May 11, 1941, there were less frequent German air raids on London (the most notable one on July 27, 1941) until the Little Blitz began on January 21, 1944 (through April 19, 1944), followed by V-1 "doodlebugs" and V-2 rockets that continued into 1945. The period from May 11, 1941 to January 21, 1944 was known as the "Lull."

Accordingly, the historical figures who appear in *Last Train to Gidleigh* — from Prime Minister Winston Churchill and Home Secretary Herbert Morrison to National Fire Service Chief of the Fire Staff and Inspector-in-Chief Aylmer Firebrace and Harry Rethoret (General Manager of the Fire Underwriters' Investigation Bureau of Canada, Inc. and author of the treatises *Arson, Fraud & Perjury* (1938) and *Fire Investigation* (1945)) — neither said nor did what is set forth here.

However, Alvar Lidell's Pearl Harbor announcement on the BBC is accurate. And Dame Agatha Christie did give an interview in 1967 that included the following exchange:

> *"In your novel* The Murder of Roger Ackroyd *it is only in the end discovered that the character who is telling the story in first person — is a killer. What can be the next step? Somebody said that it remains only that the killer is — a reader!"*

> *"Yes, that would be a really good idea," she smiled cheerfully, glittering eyes from behind glasses sank into wrinkles, her long teeth shined. "Certainly it would be. But how to do this?"*

Richard Weill, a practicing lawyer and former prosecutor, is a member of the Dramatists Guild.

His legal thriller *Framed* premiered in Oxnard, California in 2016 to standing-room-only audiences, a run extended by popular demand, and critical acclaim ("The script is engaging, entertaining, highly credible, and well worth your time. ... the script bears an uncommon authenticity, as well as being literate, concise and cogent." *Ventura Breeze*, May 11, 2016; "Weill's courtroom experience is evident in both the attorneys' background discussions and in the snippets of trial scenes" in a play that "offers a killer performance that will keep audience guessing," *Ventura County Star*, May 13, 2016). On the second anniversary of *Framed*'s Oxnard opening, Sidney Books released Mr. Weill's fascinating account of the play's eight-year journey from conception to the page to the stage: *We Open in Oxnard Saturday Afternoon*.

Mr. Weill's play *Sisters*, suggested by an unsolved 1966 murder, moves backwards scene-by-scene to tell the story of how a crime changed a prominent family — and why.

Besides *Sisters* and *Framed*, Mr. Weill has written a fictional version of Agatha Christie's 1926 disappearance (*Imperfect Alibi*), a comedy-drama set in 1950's New York about the 23-year collaboration of two mystery writers (*Hardbound*); a thriller about adultery and betrayal (*The Other Woman*), a two-character thriller (*Seed of Doubt*), and an evening of three short plays about crime and crime writers (*Constant Companions*).

Mr. Weill also has written two plays about young artists (*Emergence of the Soul; The Unframed Canvas*), a political comedy (*Another County Heard From*), a one-man play (*This ... Is Murrow*), an allegory about baseball's Black Sox scandal (*And the Echo Answered Fraud*), a play set in the New York Civil Jail (*This Little World*), a musical version of *Waiting for Godot* (*The Vaudevillians*), and a screenplay about a baseball broadcaster (*The Voice of Summer*).

Last Train to Gidleigh is his first novel.